T0157178

Design *of a* Dream

J.M.Holden

iUniverse, Inc.
New York Bloomington

Design of a Dream

iUniverse books may be ordered through booksellers or by contacting:

iUniverse
1663 Liberty Drive
Bloomington, IN 47403
www.iuniverse.com
1-800-Authors (1-800-288-4677)

ISBN: 978-1-4502-2514-4 (pbk)
ISBN: 978-1-4502-2515-1 (ebook)

Printed in the United States of America

iUniverse rev. date: 4/14/10

— CHAPTER 1 —

In a small east coast town, just outside Connecticut, on a quiet tree lined street, in a workshop full of fabric and sketches thrown everywhere trying to get ready for the fall line fashion show. In the middle of the entire bustle was a petite, dark haired woman with a pencil sticking out of her hair. She was talking on her phone while giving instructions to all the people around her. "Sam, did you hear me?" A tall well built man in a tuxedo was trying to get her attention. She turned to him and hung up her phone. "Yes I heard you, and I am trying to finish so we can go." They smiled at each other with undying admiration in their eyes. Samantha Naples was a top designer in the country and her life had never been better than it was at this very moment. Her career was soaring and her private life was bringing levels of joy she never knew existed.

Sam began her career from a small one bedroom apartment with a table top sewing machine that she bought at a yard sale. She sketched and stitched all night working towards her dream of being a fashion designer and worked at the corner deli during the day.

It was a small place with four tables and five stools at the lunch bar and people liked the food. The deli was always busy with businessmen and women rushing to grab a quick lunch before their next appointment. They were all cordial while they talked on there phones and ordered their lunches, but then they were gone till the next day. The owner was a sweet man with the happiest eyes Sam had ever seen, Dominic; he took care of Sam like a daughter. His wife Constance was a beautiful woman who turned heads just walking across the room, she was slender, with long red hair and the grace of an angel. They were so in love with each other and with their life they could not wait till they had their own children to share it with. Dominic was older than Constance, but they agreed to wait till the deli was a success and that time was coming soon.

Sam had worked there since it opened four years ago and she was the only employee. She was friendly and polite and always remembered what people liked. While working Sam noticed what women were wearing and had ideas how to change almost everything they wore. She would grab her sketchbook during her break and put ideas on paper.

Constance watched her sketch to see her ideas and she loved them all. "Sam, you will be a great success one day and I will wear your designs proudly". It was that encouragement that kept Sam going and working so hard. She loved Dominic and Constance so much she could not imagine leaving them, but they all knew one day it would happen.

One typical spring day as the usual customers came in the deli, sandwiches and drinks were going out the door as fast as the customers were coming in, and all but one of them was familiar. A tall dark haired man, very well built with the bluest eyes and brightest smile dressed in jeans and a black shirt. Suddenly Dominic let out a holler that stopped everything and everyone, "Oh my, it can't be.....my baby brother, Nicholas, is it really you?" He was so over whelmed that he ran out front and hugged this man with tears in both their eyes and smiles bright enough to light up the darkest sky. Constance just stood in shock and amazement; she could not believe what she was seeing. "Nicholas?" she screeched and ran to him. Every customer was smiling and greeting this man like they knew him. It was not a big community, everyone knew everyone and Dominic and Constance were well liked. Sam just kept on working and not paying much attention to this stranger, with his strong broad shoulders and slender waist.

She tried not to stare at his crystal blue eyes and his full head of dark wavy hair. He was the most gorgeous man she had ever seen and he had a smile that made her knees weak. Constance brought Nicholas to the back to meet Sam. "Hello it is pleasure to meet you Sam, Dom and Connie have told me so much about you." Sam smiled and shook his hand, excused herself shyly and went back to work. She was shaken by this man; his looks and his physique were very intimidating to her. She had never seen a man that shook her to the core like him. Sam kept her composure and finished the lunch crowd's orders, while Dominic and Constance visited with Nicholas. When the customers were all gone and the deli was quiet Sam grabbed a cold drink and proceeded to clean up the counter and tables. She could hear Connie and Dom laughing in the back and smiled to herself for their happiness. When she finished cleaning up she went to the back room and began to say her good-byes for the day but Connie would not hear of her leaving yet "Please stay a bit and visit with Nick. He has come all the way from California to see us and you are family too." Sam blushed and agreed to stay a little while. Dom and Connie started cooking for the next day's menu and told stories about their family.

They all laughed and enjoyed their visit, Sam tried very hard not to stare or get to close to this stranger, she knew she would look like a school girl if she did and did not want him to think he had that kind of power over her. Sam had a plan for her life and it did not include any man, especially one like Nicholas Naples, tall, dark and alluring. He watched her every move and smiled at her often, she was becoming very unsettled by him, fidgeting in her chair trying to appear uninterested. Who did this man think he was, she had no intention of letting him get close to her, no man would ever get close to her again, and she was not going to weaken not even for this gorgeous man next to her. She noticed how late it was getting and she had work to do so Sam excused herself and left for the night. As she walked the two blocks to her apartment all she could think about was him and his piercing eyes. She had to admit to herself that his charming manner was hard to resist but she was better than that, she was not some innocent girl with a crush, she was sure he thought she would fall all over him, "I'm sure most woman do." She told herself. Just because he is tall, extremely well built, model handsome and has a low seductive voice, she was stronger than that, "he was just another man, nothing special." She walked into her apartment so involved with her thoughts about him she never heard her neighbor say hello to her. She made herself some coffee, trying to dismiss all thoughts of Nicholas Naples. Sam did not get much work done that night, in fact she did not sleep well either, every time she closed her eyes all she could see was him. She finally convinced herself he was just Dom's brother nothing more and it would stay that way.

— CHAPTER 2 —

When she got to the deli the next morning, Dom called to her from the backroom. "Sam, would you come to the house tonight for dinner? Connie and I are having a small get together for Nick and we want you there." Sam tried to think of any reason to get out of this without hurting their feelings but she came up with nothing, so she smiled and hesitantly accepted the invitation. The day went as usual, busy and fast, when she finished her work, still trying to think of a way to get out of this invitation, she went into the back room and told Dom she had a lot of work to do on her designs so she would not be able to make their party. He smiled, "Please come Little One you are like a daughter to me and I really want to have my whole family there." she finally gave in, how could she refuse him, he had been wonderful to her. Sam left to go home and get ready for the dinner party. She tried on everything in her closet and finally decided to wear something she designed, a royal blue cowl neck halter dress and wrap with matching shoes and purse.

She picked out a necklace and earring set her mother had left to her when she died, it was silver hearts and diamonds. She let her dark slightly curled hair fall around her shoulders to outline her face. When she looked in the mirror she was pleased with what she saw, "Why should I worry about how I look, I am not going to impress anyone." She dabbed on some perfume, talking to herself all the way out the door, "this is just a dinner party at my bosses' house, nothing more."

The cab was on time which irritated Sam; they are always late why they were on time tonight, a night she would rather have stayed home. As the cab pulled up to the modest tutor style home, Connie came out to greet her. "My don't you look beautiful, Sam" she said with a very pleased smile. As Sam was escorted to the living room she noticed that she and Nicholas were the only ones there. Dom came in with drinks for them and quickly left the room. Nick was looking at Sam, he could not believe how beautiful she was and finally spoke after what seemed an eternity of silence to Sam, "My God you are gorgeous Samantha". Sam blushed like a school girl; she turned away from him trying to act uncaring, "thank-you" she said softly.

Connie and Dom finally came to the living room, laughing and hugging as usual. Dom raised his glass "To my wife, the most wonderful woman in the world". They all drank to his toast and Sam knew there was something going on by the giddiness of Connie. "What's going on?" she whispered to her, Connie rubbed her belly telling her that their dream of having a family is beginning. Sam was so excited that she squealed with joy and hugged her. Dom could no longer be quiet he jumped up and yelled "I am going to be a father!" Everyone was so excited they all hugged each other, when she and Nick hugged they just looked into each others eyes and smiled at each other. Sam had to excuse herself to the bathroom; she needed to compose herself after being so close to him. Sam could not figure out what was happening to her she was acting like she had never been with a man before. Well at least not one like him, he was a dangerous kind of man, gorgeous, charming, intimidating as hell, yet seemed gentle and kind. Sam made sure she was composed and told herself she was not going to fall for this guy, no matter what, she had dreams to fulfill which did not include him.

The dinner was wonderful and very drawn out, Sam was anxious to leave and get away from Nick and his alluring ways. Connie was concerned about how withdrawn Sam was acting and Dom was so overwhelmed about the baby he didn't notice anything. Nick tried to talk to Sam and she only nodded and gave one word answers. She couldn't even make eye contact with him; she had to prove to him she was not interested. As the evening went on she was thinking of any excuse to leave but nothing was acceptable, how could she be so selfish on such a special evening for Connie and Dom, after all they had done for her. So she decided to stay for a bit longer, convincing herself it was for them. After dinner they went out to the gazebo in the back yard Dom and Connie excused themselves and went inside, they wanted to give Nick and Sam time alone. They were hoping something special would happen between the two of them, they were perfect for each other, at least Dom and Connie thought so. It was a beautiful night, cool enough for her to wear her wrap, which she was glad of; she was nervous being alone with this stranger and it gave her something to do with her hands. As she stood looking at the stars and

moon praying for a reason to leave she felt a hand on her shoulder "Would you like to sit down, Samantha?" she nodded and he guided her to a loveseat style swing. He sat with her and they both looked up at the stars. "Are they not the most beautiful things you have ever seen?" Sam just nodded. "You are a woman of few words, are you always this quiet?" Sam nodded. Nick looked at her with question in his eyes, "Have I offended you Samantha?" Sam shook her head, she tried to look away from him but she was drawn to him and had no control over it. "I just don't know what to think of you." He smiled and gave her a gentle kiss on the hand. "What do you want from me?" she asked, he laughed out loud and told her "I just want to get to know the woman that my family thinks so much of." She smiled thinking of Connie and Dom, how wonderful they are to her. "I love them like family too. How long are you planning to visit for?" He smiled at her, which about made her melt in her seat, "I will be here for as long as it takes." With that he stood up and walked to the edge of the gazebo. She wanted to ask what he meant but didn't, why should she care about anything this man had to say he was nothing to her. The night was getting cooler and Sam noticed it was getting late, "I have to call a cab, it is late and I have work to do tonight, please excuse me." Nick turned and watched her walk back to the house and disappear into the night. He smiled to himself, "How challenging yet wonderful this was all going to be." he thought.

It wasn't long before the cab arrived and Sam was on her way to the security of her little apartment and her much loved work. Even though she knew it was never going to be anything she still could not get Nick out of her mind. Why was this man so intriguing to her? She has never bothered to think twice about any man that she had met, she has no room in her life for any man especially him and of that she was certain.

— CHAPTER 3 —

The next morning as Sam walked to the work she saw a black limousine parked in front of the deli. She wondered who could be in that car and why they were at the deli, as she walked she dismissed the thought and her mind turned to Nick again. She tossed and turned all night because of him, telling her self it was nothing and to just forget him, he was not in her plans. When she opened the door to the deli she stopped in shock to see who was at the counter, it was Stephen, her brother. He turned to her with a sad look in his eyes, "Samantha, I have been waiting for you" he hugged her and asked her to sit down. Stephen was older than Sam and very successful in business, thanks to her father, he never liked how Sam lived and always wanted her to change her ways. Sam was sure this was another ploy on his part to get her to accept her family's lifestyle. She never imagined what he was really there for, "Samantha, you need to come home, for awhile, Dad is sick and he is asking to see you." Sam was silent for a moment, "What is it? Is he dying?" Stephen just lowered his head, she knew what that meant.

She stood up and went in the back to talk to Connie and Dom. They were very understanding and sympathetic to Sam and told her to take all the time she needed. "I won't be gone long; at least I don't think so." Sam came out and told Stephen she needed to get some things together and she would be back. As Sam ran to her apartment, she was panic stricken about going back home, she knew there was no good to come of this trip but she had to go.

When she returned to the deli she found Stephen sitting and talking to Nick. She was so absorbed in what she had to do she forgotten all about him. Stephen shook his hand and helped Sam with her bags, she hugged Connie and Dom with tears in her eyes, and she had never been away from them since she met them. When she turned around Nick was looking at her with concern and told her to have a safe trip and don't worry about the deli he was going to fill in for her. She quickly thanked him and went out to the limo where Stephen was waiting for her.

On the way to the airport all she could think about was what may be waiting for her back home in Atlanta, a place she never thought she would have to see again. She left four years ago, it felt like a lifetime. She shuttered to think of David, what would she do if she saw him again? He was her first love and her last, He broke her heart and her spirit, and he was not someone she ever wanted to see again. All the pain of her past came rushing to the surface, everything she had endured at the hands of David and her mother. "God, please don't let him find me" she prayed to herself. Her Dad was sick and she needed to concentrate on that.

As the plane landed she turned into the old Samantha, conservative, cold and arrogant, not someone she liked to be, but it was just the way she had to be when she was home, it was expected of her. The limo pulled through the gates of her family estate and she was preparing herself for what she was about to see, at least she thought she could. When she walked in the front door she saw Margie, their housekeeper and always Sam's confidant growing up. She looked worried and had aged some, they hugged, "Welcome home Miss Sam" the woman whispered to her, she took Sam's bags up to her old room. Sam had almost forgotten how big the house was and decorated to a tea, her mother saw to that, fine china displayed in the dining room and all Dads' trophies were displayed in the study. Expensive paintings line the walls of the living room and porcelain figurines were on every table and shelf. Oriental rugs lay on the floors in every room with matching draperies. Nothing had changed it was just as it was when she left right after her mothers funeral. She remembered her mothers' way of decorating, always the best and nothing less would do, she was a perfectionist in everything she did, and Sam hated that about her. As she went up the stairs she ran her hand on the banister remembering how she and Stephen used to slide down it as children just to irritate their mother. At the top of the stairs was the bench seat in the bay window that she spent many hours looking out of.

This house was her prison as a child and when she left she swore she would never come back. But, Dad was sick and she had to be there for him, no matter what. He was her hero, always there for her with a hug or a smile. She was his baby girl and everyone knew it, especially her mother, she was jealous of the relationship between Sam and her father. But Sam didn't care he was her dad and her best friend. She always imagined she would find a man like him, but after David she stopped looking.

Sam walked into her old room, it was the same, nothing had changed. She opened the window and just looked out on to the grounds that she used to play on as a child. The dogwood trees she planted with her father as a child were in full bloom, they were his favorite tree, hers too. So many fond memories, yet so much pain still echoing in her heart.

Sam showered and got dressed to see her father, she wore jeans and a sweater, Dad was not a fancy guy. He always wore jeans when he came home from work, mother fussed at him constantly for it, she was worried someone would come by and see him dressed so shabby. He would just dismiss the whole thing and continue reading the paper. As she walked to his room she could hear the oxygen machine pumping and a woman was speaking to him. When she opened the door she was amazed at what she saw. He was in bed with tubes coming out of his arms and mouth, not what she expected but then what should she expect. He was always a strong man, built like a man half his age, he worked hard and was kind to everyone he met. This was not the man she remembered, he was frail and helpless. The woman in the room told him Samantha was there, he opened his eyes and smiled at her. He held out his hand for Sam to hold and she slowly walked to his bedside and took it. She leaned over him and kissed him on the cheek, "Hello Dad." He had tears in his eyes when he looked at her; she smiled at him and rubbed his cheek. The woman excused herself and quietly closed the door. "She's a good nurse, Sam"

He always called her 'Sam' another thing her mother disliked. Sam's face relaxed "How are you feeling Dad?" He grinned "It's not so bad honi; the medicine helps keep the pain down." She wanted to cry, but she knew if she did it would upset him so she just kept talking so she wouldn't. "Stephen told me you wanted to see me, is there something you wanted from me, Dad?"

He struggled to inhale, looked at his baby girl with all the love he had always had for her. "Sam, I am not going to be here much longer and I need to know you are ok, are you ok, Sam?" he asked her with a raspy voice. She nodded her head "I am fine Dad, I have a good life, a job I love and my designs are coming along. Don't worry about me I am fine." "I do worry about you, Sam, you are so stubborn and head strong I know you would never ask for anything, but I have made provisions for you in my will just in case you ever feel you need it. And I won't take no for an answer. You are my daughter and I will take care of you one way or another." "But Dad I don't need anything, I work hard and I have all I need." He smiled at her "My baby girl, always so independent never did like being rich, did you?" Sam just shook her head and began to cry, "Dad, I am so sorry I have been gone so long but, I just couldn't come home, you understand don't you?" He nodded and closed his eyes, "You were always the one to do what you wanted and no one was going to change your mind....not even me, I have missed you Sam." She kissed his hand, "Dad you get some rest and I will be back in a while, I love you Dad."

He waved weakly at her as she left his room. Sam walked back to her room full of despair, how could this happen to him, the one man she always looked up to, the one man who never hurt her or made her cry. Sam was beside herself with grief, she didn't know what to do with all the emotions churning inside her.

It was different when mother died; she was not a loving, warm person. They were never close, Sam was a tomboy and her mother was a materialistic debutant, she never understood Sam and never tried. Stephen was her favorite; he loved material things and everything that goes with being rich, Sam hated having to act like a proper young lady. Her father let her be herself, climbing trees, riding horses, finding frogs in the pond and he would laugh when she brought them in to show her mother. Now Stephen is running Dad's businesses and living the life they were both groomed to live. Not Sam she was not going to be like her mother or Stephen, she was her father's daughter through and through and dam proud of it.

The doorbell broke her thoughts; she heard a man's voice she did not recognize. She went down stairs to greet the visitor; a short, stocky man with a briefcase was standing in the entranceway. He smiled at

Sam "Hello Miss, you must be Samantha, I am John Collins; I'd like to speak with Stephen please." Sam nodded and went to get Stephen, "Stephen, there is a man to see you, John Collins?" "Oh yes, finally." Stephen hurried to the door and escorted Mr. Collins to the study. They were in the study for what seemed like hours when the doors finally opened, Stephen called to Sam to join them. "Samantha this is father's attorney he has some papers for you to sign," he gave Sam with a hateful look, and she read the papers Mr. Collins handed her, she quickly read them, signed them, handed them back to the attorney and left the room. When Mr. Collins left, Sam went into the study, "Stephen what will happen to Dad's businesses?" He glared at her just like her mother used to, "You were never interested in the family business before what do you care now?" Sam was insulted and hurt, to think her own brother is going to treat her like she was not part of the family, just like her mother.

Anger filled the room, she hated all that Stephen stood for, money, power and the arrogance he showed, Sam went outside to cool off and think. She was not here for Stephen; she was here for her father and only him, to hell with Stephen and his attitude towards her. It was getting close to dinner time so Sam went up to her room and changed into one of her favorite dresses, green taffeta with white chiffon accents, she looked as expected to and hated every minute of it.

As she entered the dining room Stephen smiled at her "Nice to see you still know how to dress for dinner." The butler pulled out her chair and nodded at her in approval. Stephen sat in her father's chair which made her angry. "Daddy's not even gone yet and you are just taking over aren't you?" "Someone had to do it and you obviously don't want to and never did" with that the rest of the dinner was silent, Sam was so exhausted she excused herself and went to bed.

The next morning when Sam woke she heard people talking in the hall; she opened her door, Margie and Stephen were having a disagreement. "Miss Sam, I am so sorry for waking you." "It's ok Margie, what's going on?" Stephen dismissed Margie "Samantha, we need to talk, meet me downstairs?" Sam grabbed her robe, and went down the stairs she heard a woman talking to Stephen in the study. As Sam entered the room they went silent, Stephen took the woman's hand. "Samantha, this is Victoria Steel, my fiancé" Sam smiled at her and shook her hand "How wonderful Stephen, your getting married, when?" Stephen shook his head and rubbed his hands together "Samantha, we are to be married on Saturday, but I don't think it is appropriate considering what's going on with father." Sam agreed. "Why can't she talk to your father and see if he would mind if we still went through with the wedding, he won't say no to his precious Sam." Victoria smirked.

With daggers in her eyes Sam looked at Stephen in total disbelief. "You want me to talk to Daddy about your wedding when he is on his death bed, have you lost all your senses?" Stephen tried to explain that the invitations and everything has been set for weeks and it would cost a fortune to reschedule everything, Sam knew he was doing this for his precious Victoria who sat looking at the enormous ring on her hand and smiled at Sam like a viper waiting to strike. "I will not talk to Daddy about this or anything else for either of you and don't ask me again!" Sam stormed out of the room and went to the courtyard to calm herself before going to see her father. "How could he marry someone so cold and uncaring? She is just like mother that's how, just what he loved about mother he loves about Victoria." She muttered to her self. "Well he is on his own."

Sam went back in the house and headed up to her fathers room, as she entered she saw him sitting in his chair by the window overlooking the courtyard. He must have seen Sam out there and he knows she only goes out there when she is very upset and troubled. He turned his head toward her as she came in and smiled, with his hand out he asked her to come and sit by him. Sam sat with him for hours just looking at the courtyard, remembering all the things they did together when she was a child.

When he finally fell asleep she left the room, she went to her room and dressed for the day then headed to the kitchen. Margie was there as usual making preparations for lunch. "May I have some coffee, Margie?" Margie stopped what she was doing and got Sam coffee and scones, she made them for her when she was little and knew she would love to have some. Sam thanked her and sat at the table thinking, "Margie, sit with me." Margie sat and waited for her to speak. "Margie, what do you think of this Victoria?" Margie hesitated to answer; Sam knew by the look on Margie's face she did not like this woman. "That's ok, I understand, you don't have to say a word." With that she went back to work and Sam finished her coffee.

The kitchen was always the room to talk and think about things, Margie was always there to listen and comfort Sam, and they were very close. Just as Sam was getting her thoughts straight, Stephen walked in and asked her to reconsider their request. Sam turned away from him and drank the last of her coffee, put the cup down, walked over to him and slapped him, "Don't ever ask me to do something so unspeakable again!" When she left the room Stephen asked Margie to speak to her and try to convince her to do it, Margie looked at him with disgust in her eyes "I cannot sir, I am sorry." Stephen was so upset with Sam he stormed out of the room.

Sam headed up the stairs to sit on the bench seat and think, with tears running down her face she tried to figure out how Stephen could treat her father like that. The man has given everything to him his whole life and now Stephen is repaying him by disrespecting him in his final hours for a woman like Victoria, just another reminder that her mother is still around and making things impossible for her. Well Sam was not going to let Stephen and Victoria upset her fathers last days.

With determination and stubbornness that is so Sam she went into the study and confronted both of them. "I cannot do as you ask and I will not allow either of you to do this to Dad, so just cancel all your plans and do this at another time. I will not stand by and watch you be so cold and heartless to the man who has given you everything. Stephen you are so much your mother's son it makes me sick and as soon as Dads' affairs are settled I am leaving this house and you will never hear from me again!" She turned and left them both stunned and appalled that she would speak to them that way. Victoria looked at Stephen with contempt "You will do something about her, and I mean now!" Stephen just stood there looking at the door his little sister just went through. Sam felt good about it she knew she had to do it for her father's sake and had no regrets.

— CHAPTER 4 —

She went upstairs to check on her father. She opened his door and he was back in bed, he waved her in and smiled at the sight of her. "You look gorgeous baby girl." "Thank-you Daddy, Can I get you anything?" He shook his head slowly, trying not to show her the pain he was in. "Sam, I have to tell you one thing before I die, I have always loved you and hoped you would find a love that would fill the emptiness in your life." "But Dad I have a very full life" "No Sam you don't, you shut down after David, you need love to complete you and give you joy, please Sam find the man you are meant to love and hold on for dear life, you deserve it Baby Girl." Sam was crying uncontrollably now, her father took his last breath smiling at her. Sam stayed with him, crying on his chest until the nurse came in and found her. "I am so sorry; he was a wonderful man, one of a kind."

Sam left the room and went to the dining room to find Stephen. When she walked in Stephen started yelling at her about the way she spoke in front of Victoria until he noticed the look on her face. "Oh my god, Samantha, is he......gone?" Sam nodded and broke down crying again. Stephen ran up the stairs to his father's room in disbelief, yelling "NO...FATHER NO!" When he got to his room he saw it was true, he ran to the bed and hugged his fathers still body, crying and sobbing.

The funeral was on a grey day with very little wind. Stephen and Victoria stood together like statues, cold and hard. Sam tried to hold in her grief while standing arm in arm with Margie, next to the grave site. Everyone who ever knew him was there, most of them Sam had never met. Her mother's funeral was no where near as crowded with mourners. The service was short but that's how he wanted it he was not one for long drawn out good byes.

Sam walked up to the casket and put a single red rose on it, Margie held on to her as she walked away, Stephen and Victoria just walked away. Back at the house, people filled every room, talking about how wonderful he was and what a loss it was. Margie kept stopping to check on Sam, She knew it was hardest on her, "Miss Sam can I get you anything?" Sam just declined her gestures, at the end of the day, Sam went to her room to collect her things to leave when she heard a knock on her door, "May I come in, Samantha?" Sam nodded through her tears. "Samantha, I am sorry for your loss, but could you stay a few more days for the wedding?" Sam turned to her with all the strength she could come up with "Have you lost your mind? I would not be here if it was not for my father and you think I want to stay to watch you and Stephen get married, just days after we buried him, GET OUT AND STAY OUT!" She pushed her out the door and slammed it behind her. Sam was so distraught she fell on the floor and cried until she had no more tears.

All her bags were packed and down by the door, Margie was waiting to say good bye to her. Sam came down the stairs knowing this was the last time she would ever see her friend and confidant. The two women hugged and cried till the cab pulled up and her bags were loaded into the trunk. "I will never forget you Margie, take care of yourself." the woman nodded wiping her eyes. Stephen never came to say good bye and that was fine with her, she was keeping her vow of never seeing him again after the funeral. The cab pulled out as Margie watched her friend leave for the final time; she went back inside to face the cold, empty house again.

The flight was long and Sam was so anxious to get back to her life she was fidgety in her seat. Now that her Dad was gone she would never have to go back home again. Her past got buried with him at least she thought it did. Just then she heard someone say her name. "Samantha, Samantha Trent?" it was David; he was sitting in the seat across from her. She glared at him, her fears of seeing him had come to life, "I have nothing to say to you David, leave me alone." She turned away from him and he moved into the seat closer to her. "Samantha, I heard you were home, sorry to hear about your father, he was a great businessman." Sam knew it was all false sentiment on his part, her father warned him to stay away from Sam after she told him what David had done to her. "You have no right to talk to me about my father or anything else." She turned her back to him for the rest of the flight. He grinned at her behind her back knowing he would see her again, sooner than she thought.

Sam waited for him to leave the plane before she got out of her seat, giving him time to get far ahead of her. As the luggage rack went around she found her bags and when she reached for them an arm went in front of her "I've got these" It was Nick. "Dom asked me to pick you up, and I hope you don't mind?" Sam smiled nervously at him, she was so glad he was here, but she was not going to let him know that. They walked to the car, put her bags in the trunk and proceeded to get in the car. Nick opened her door, stopped and pulled Sam to him, "I am so sorry about your father, Samantha if you ever want to talk I will listen" Sam was taken by surprise, she held on to him like he would disappear if she let go. When she finally let go he smiled at her and helped her into the car.

They drove in silence all the way to the deli, "Connie gave me instruction to bring you straight here, I'm sorry." "It's ok I am kind of looking forward to seeing them." Before he could even get the car in park, Dom and Connie were at Sam's door opening it and pulling her to them. They missed her so much; they felt so bad for what she had gone through. They hugged her and kissed her cheeks like parents seeing their child for the first time. It took Sam's breath away, but it was just what she needed. Nick carried her bags into the deli, Dom and Connie led Sam in arm in arm. "It feels so good to be home, I missed you so much. I hope I never have to leave again."

They sat and talked, she told them all about her father, the house and Stephen and Victoria. They sat in amazement and disbelief that someone could be so cold and uncaring. Nick had made some sandwiches and brought some drinks to the table while listening to Sam. How could such a wonderful woman have so much pain and heartache in her life? Dom and Connie listened intently; this was the first time Sam had ever spoken of her family. They did not try to stop her, even after 2 hours of listening; they felt she needed to talk and they loved her so much they let her. Finally, Nick spoke up "I think Sam could use some rest, I will take her home and we can all continue this in the morning?" Sam agreed and hugged them good-bye. When they got to her door, Sam took out her keys and unlocked it; she turned to him "Would you like to bring those in for me?" He smiled arms full of luggage and walked in to her small but comfortable apartment.

He set the luggage down and looked around at all the sketches and fabrics, "Wow you have been busy." Sam was making coffee and smiled at his remark. "Coffee?" He was so engrossed in her designs he did not hear her. "Nick, coffee?" He just nodded his head and kept examining her sketches. This woman is more than he ever thought; beautiful, talented, hard working and intelligent he was in awe of her. Sam gave him his cup and smiled at his obvious interest in her work. "Like them?" "Are you kidding these are absolutely the most beautiful designs I have ever seen." "And you are an expert how?" He had never told her anything about himself, "I own a design house in California, I am always looking for new designers." Sam was in shock, "You what?" He turned to her and smiled, "Yes Sam, I own a design house, didn't Dom tell you?" She could not speak she just shook her head. Nick laughed, "And I thought that was why you would not talk to me because you knew what I do for a living." "No, I had no idea he said nothing to me." "Maybe he wanted us to discover all this on our own; they are hopeless romantics you know." They both laughed and drank coffee and Sam explained her designs to him and he was totally involved in every word coming out of her full pink lips. Sam was so proud to be showing her work she lost all track of time, when they finally stopped talking it was after midnight, Sam yawned and Nick realized how tired she was "I better go and let you get some sleep, we can continue this tomorrow." With that she agreed and walked him to the door, She thanked him and he kissed her cheek, "Good night Samantha" Sam smiled and closed the door.

Did this really happen, did she really show her designs to a man that not only is gorgeous and charming but also owns a design house, and why didn't Dom or Connie tell her anything about this? What did they have planned for her? Well she was not going to let them manipulate her into anything, especially a relationship with Nick. Sam sat drinking her coffee; she was too fired up to sleep even though she was exhausted so she began sketching until she fell asleep with the pencil and pad in her hand.

— CHAPTER 5 —

The alarm went off as usual but this was not her usual day, she felt refreshed and ready to take on the world even though she only had three hours of sleep. Sam walked to work with a skip in her step and when she walked in the deli Connie came to her "So how did it go? You and Nick hit it off? Did he see your designs? Tell me." Sam laughed "I guess you could say we hit it off. Yes he saw my designs and why did you not tell me that he owns a design house?" Connie acted coy "Oh did I forget to tell you that?" They both laughed and hugged, "I am not getting involved with anyone, and I told you I have no room in my life for a man." Connie pretended to agree with her, smiling at her the whole time.

The phone ringing broke up their joking, Dom answered it," Yes she is here, Sam, it's for you" Sam took the phone "Hello" "Sam? It's Nick are you busy after work today?" She smiled at Connie who was watching her closely, "No why?" "I want to show you something if you are willing" Sam hesitated, "I guess so, what time?" "Six ok?" "See you then" Sam hung up the phone and started to work, Dom and Connie stood waiting for her to explain that call. Sam let them wonder for as long as she could. "That was Nick; he wants to take me to see something after work." They both beamed with joy for her, "You said yes right?" "Of course!" she tried not to smile at them, they all broke out in laughter. The day was busier than usual but Sam did not mind she was so curious about what Nick had to show her after work that was all she could think about.

What could it be? Sam was so intrigued she almost felt excited, Connie and Dom were so hopeful for her and Nick, but they had to let nature take it's course, they didn't want to push, they knew if they did Sam would back off from him completely.

At 6 o'clock sharp a car pulled up in front of the deli, Sam about jumped out of her seat when he walked in. "Are you ready Sam?" "I have been all day." The two of them walked out to the car, "I hope you like surprises." "I do" Sam looked up at him with curiosity. The words her father told her kept running through her head as she watch him out of the corner of her eye. Could this be him, the one daddy told me to look for and make a life with? No, how could Daddy know about Nick?

No, he couldn't have, but then maybe he saw something in my eyes that gave it away, am I kidding myself about how I feel about him? No I can't fall for him I have a plan and I am certain I don't have time for love. Maybe I should make time and see where it goes; she smiled to herself just as the car came to a stop in front of the biggest building on the block.

"Well, Samantha, we're here, what do you think?" Sam got out of the car and stood looking up and around this massive structure. "What do I think of what?" "I bought it, to manufacture your designs in." Sam was dumbfounded, standing there with her mouth hanging open while Nick opened the door for her. "Are you coming?" She walked slowly toward him and into the building, still not speaking. It was huge and empty; there were two elevators, one at each side of the entrance. The windows were bigger than she had ever seen with a staircase right in the middle leading up to a second level. It had to be four stories tall. "What do you mean this is to manufacture my designs?" "Sam, I have talked to Dom and Connie and they agree with me that it is time for you to make your designs and sell them. So I bought this building and I want you to make your designs here." Sam stared at him like she had never seen him before, "But I don't know how to go about all this." Nick grinned "I do and I will help you every step of the way." Sam thought about it for a long time walking around in silence; she turned to him and smiled, "Ok what's in it for you?" He laughed out loud, "I was hoping you would allow my name to be on the building, I have always wanted a design house on the east coast but never had a designer to run it. Your designs are exquisite,

Sam, and I want to help you become the most famous designer in the world. Ok?" Sam contemplated this for a few minutes, "So we would be partners, in business, your name and my designs?" "Basically, all I would be is the house your designs are made in and your name would go on every piece you put out of here. I would not make a dime off your talent, just stand by and watch you take the fashion world by storm." Sam could not believe this was all happening; he is too good to be true. Sam took one last look and walked to the door, "I can't accept this, it is all wonderful but, I could not ask anyone to take that kind of a risk on me. Especially you, if I failed I could never forgive myself." She went out to the car and waited for him.

He got in the car and turned to her "Sam what in the world would make you think you would fail?" Sam just sighed "I just don't know if I'm that good." They drove back to the deli in silence; Dom and Connie were waiting in the door like doting parents. "Well, what did you think, isn't it wonderful? Sam?" Sam ran into the back room, she was so beside herself she couldn't even talk to them. Nick told them what happened, "She is scared, I understand, but I have seen her work it is some of the best I have ever seen. I think I better back off for a bit and let her think about it. I am going back to California in the morning, take care of some things there and I will return in a couple of weeks. I will see you in the morning before I leave."

As he walked out Dom shook his head in disbelief, "Sam, please come out here." he called to her. Sam approached him like a child being punished, "Yes Dom" he eyed her up and down for a minute and told her to sit down with him. Dominic was a very good business man and Sam trusted him completely. He talked to her about what Nicholas had planned, the whole idea of opening a design house here was his, and he just needed a designer so when he came here they told him about Sam. He explained that the whole idea of buying the building was already in the works before they met. "Sam please think about this, it is your dream and we want you to have it." Sam sat quietly thinking, Connie came out of the back with a very worried face, "Sam don't let this chance pass by, please and you never know what will happen till you try." Sam got up from the chair," I have to go home I will see you both in the morning."

As she walked home all she could do was cry, here she had a chance to do what she always wanted and she is too scared to take it. And what of Nick, was she just a business interest, was there more to it or had she imagined the attraction between them.

Nick said his good-byes to his brother and Connie, it was early yet and Sam was not there. "I will be back, tell Sam I said good-bye and I hope to see you all soon." As he walked out the door Connie ran after him and hugged him, "It will all work out." He smiled and drove away. He was very distracted on the flight back to California, he could only think of Sam and how much he would miss her. With a heavy heart he flew in silence, trying to think of other things but she was always there. Her beautiful brown eyes and a smile that melted his heart, he closed his eyes and imagined holding her petite body next to him. He had fallen for this quiet, talented woman, not what he planned but he had.

Upon arrival at his home he unlocked the door to the emptiness, threw his keys on the table and lay on the couch. He let his mind wonder thinking of what it would be like to kiss Sam, to make love to her, it engulfed him so much that by the time he realized what time it was the whole day had passed. He called his office to let them know he was back and would be in shortly.

After a shower and some coffee, he called Connie to let them know he got home safe. "Sam is here would you like to talk to her Nicholas?" "I can't right now, maybe next time. I have to go, talk to you soon, bye." He hung up wishing he could have talked to Sam but it would only make things harder for him. As he prepared for work he was still distracted by Sam, "Dam her and her pride. Why couldn't she see that I only want to do this for her sake? Did I present it wrong or did she take it wrong?" he asked him self. With that he walked out of his house and slammed the door.

After being away he would have a lot of things to do at the office and he needed to clear his head before he got there, but how. This woman was more than he ever expected, beautiful, intelligent, talented and mysterious enough to make any man crazy, at least it did him. As he pulled in to the parking lot he saw some of his workers, "Morning Mr. Naples" He smiled and waved to them. He entered his office, put his briefcase down by his desk and sat checking his messages. None from her, he frowned, "Mr. Naples, can I get you anything this morning?" his secretary asked, "No thanks just the morning paper." She left his office to do as he asked; when she brought the paper to him he was facing out the window. "Did your trip go as planned Sir?" "Not exactly, Jan, but the next one will." She nodded and left him to his work.

— CHAPTER 6 —

Dom was very quiet as they prepared for the day; Connie wasn't her usual bubbly self either. She was usually glowing and excited about the new life she was carrying. When Sam arrived they all said good morning and went about the day. Sam knew something was different; the mood of the deli was very solemn. "What is going on with Dom, Connie, is he alright?" She frowned and told Sam," He is worried that Nicholas will not be back in time for the baby. He wants him to be the godfather for the baby and wants him to be here for the birth, now that you turned down his offer he may never return." Sam turned to Connie, "He will be here, and he loves you two he would never disappoint you." Connie dabbed her eyes and went back to work. Sam wondered if Nick would be back too, he told Dom he would be back soon but, what is soon, a month, a year, how long is soon? Sam was saddened to think she is the reason he left, turning him down for his offer must have insulted him. She went in back to talk to Dom, "Did I do something wrong?" He shook his head and turned away from her, he has never turned his back on her before, and Sam was shaken by this. She went back out front and tried to her job as usual; when she was done she left for the day without trying to talk to Dom again.

Her apartment was so lonely, Sam could not get over the feeling she had hurt Dom some how. She needed to make this right with him, but how? She called Connie and asked her to come over before she went home; she needed to talk to her alone, woman to woman. When Connie got there she looked tired and bewildered, "Are you ok?" Sam was concerned. "I am fine but my Dom is so sad I don't know what to do!" They sat and talked for over two hours about what to do and the two of them came up with a plan to make everyone happy.

The phone was ringing as Nick walked in the door, he ran to get it "Hello" "Nick? It's Sam." He could not believe his ears. His heart started to race and he had to take a moment to catch his breath. "Sam, is everything alright, Dom and Connie, the baby?" "Yes they are all fine, I needed to talk to you about your offer, I have thought about it and I'll do it if you are still interested." He was amazed, "I am, but if you don't mind me asking, what changed your mind?" Sam told him she talked to Dom and if he believed in her she could do it. They talked about plans to fix up the building and how to put her designs on the map, then when they both stopped talking they just laughed. "I will be there in a week, and we can finalize the whole thing." Sam beamed and agreed. "I will see you then Sam, good night" "Good night Nick." As he hung up the phone he felt his heart pounding harder than ever and he knew things were going to work out better than he thought.

Sam hung up and she and Connie clapped hands and hugged, "Everything is going to be fine now, Sam." Sam giggled, "Yes it is." Connie notice how late it was, "Sam it is late I really have to go, Dom thinks I am baby shopping, I didn't want him to know I was coming here, I will see you in the morning." "Good night Connie, be careful going home." As she watch her pull away she was so pleased with herself for what she had done, she spun around like a ballerina and laughed at herself. "Well Daddy I am going to take your advice, if this is the man I am meant to be with then so be it." and she sat in silence missing her father and remembering all he told her.

She was so lost in her thoughts she did not hear the phone ring until her machine started to talk and it was Dom. She jumped up and grabbed the receiver, "Dom, I am here what's wrong?" "Is my wife with you, Sam?" "No, she left a while ago, why?" "She is not home yet and I am worried, she said she was going baby shopping but I know she was coming to see you." Sam was concerned that something had happened to Connie on her way home, "I will go to the deli and see if she is there and call you back, and maybe she is doing some paperwork." Sam hung up and ran to the deli, but it was dark, she was not there.

Her phone was ringing when she got back, "Sam, it's me, my car broke down and I tried to call Dom but the phone is busy can you help me?" Sam was so happy to hear her voice she cried, "Connie, are you alright?" "Yes, I'm just stranded, this stupid car won't work, Dom told me to get rid of it and I wouldn't but now I guess I have too." Sam remembered all the talks and jokes about the old car she drove, "I will get a hold of him and he will be right there to get you." Sam quickly dialed Dom's number and he answered with panic in his voice, "Connie!" "No Dom, its Sam, and Connie's car broke down and won't start can you go get her?" "Of course, thank god she is safe. Thank you Sam" Sam breathed a sigh of relief that Connie was safe and would soon be home with Dominic where she belonged.

The next few days were full of anticipation and excitement waiting for Nick to return. Sam was always humming and smiling and Connie was grinning like a cat that ate the canary. Dom was getting suspicious of what they had cooked up but never let on. On the night before he was to arrive Connie could no longer hold it in she told Dom about Sam calling Nick and all the plans to be made. Dom was so overjoyed by the news he jumped up and grabbed his wife and swung her around holding her so tight she almost lost her breath.

Finally the day had arrived, Nick was coming, and Sam was like a kid at Christmas waiting for Santa. Dom and Connie decided to close early to celebrate with Nick and Sam. They cooked all afternoon and when he came through the door they all yelled with excitement. They hugged and laughed until Sam walked out from the back room, wearing an off the shoulder red dress, it was one of her designs she made to fit her like a glove. Nick could not move he was frozen by the sight of her. When she walked up to him he stood perfectly still as if she would break if he breathed. "Hello Nicholas, how was your flight?" she grinned at him and he felt his knees go weak. He grabbed a chair and sat down for a moment, "My God Sam you take my breath away." Dom roared with laughter and Nick stood up and hugged her like he would never let her go. Connie and Dom went into the back to get the food they had been preparing all day. He released Sam just enough to look at her face. "Dare I say I missed you and I can only hope you missed me as much?" "I did" He tipped her chin up to him and kissed her so gently on the mouth it made her want more. She could not believe this was happening to her, this man was everything she could ever want in her life. When Connie entered the room she knew something had happened and did not dare ask what it was as long as they were happy. Hours had passed and they had all talked and laughed so much they didn't even talk about the design house, but Sam did not care she was with the man that made her world complete and that was all that mattered for now. After cleaning and locking up the deli, Dom and Connie said their good nights and left Sam and Nick to be alone. "Would you like me to walk you home, Sam?" "I would like that very much."

As they walked down the quiet street he put his arm around her slender waist and pulled her closer to him. "It's pretty cool out tonight; I don't want you catching a chill." Sam smiled and snuggled right into his side. When they got to her door, Sam unlocked it, "Would you like to come in for something warm to break the chill of the night?" Nick was so pleased at her invitation he walked right in. Sam went into the kitchen to make some coffee while he checked out her newest sketches. Her talent amazed him, while looking at her work he watched her in the kitchen. He slowly approached her from behind; he wrapped his arms around her and buried his face in her neck. She turned around to him, looked in his eyes and kissed him with so much passion he could not help but respond with the passion he felt for her. He loved this woman with all his heart, he could not wait another minute to have her and make her his. He picked her up and carried her to the couch never letting his lips leave hers. They made love so passionately and unbridled they were both exhausted afterwards and fell asleep in each others arms. When Nick awoke he ached for her again, he kissed her awake and loved her again, she was his and they both knew it now. Her love for him was no longer a battle she was certain of that. No man had ever made her feel the way he did and no woman had ever meant to him what she does.

Sam got up from the couch and went to shower, he just lay there listening to the water running, imagining her all wet and soapy. He could not resist going to her, sneaking into the bathroom he stepped in the stream of the hot water she turned to him and kissed him again, just a passionately as the first time.

She made them breakfast and they talked about what the days events would be. Nick was meeting with contractors to go over plans for the design house; Sam was going to work at the deli. "I will meet you at the deli after my meeting and we can go over the blueprints to make sure it is what we want." Sam smiled, "I can't believe this is all happening to me, you are giving me my dream of a lifetime and I don't know how to thank you." He grinned at her, "I can think of a way." They both laughed, she kissed him and went to get dressed, and he finished his coffee and made some notes for the contractors. Sam was so happy she could barely hold it in; she pinched herself to make sure it was not a dream.

When she came out of the bedroom, Nick was on the phone, "Yes Dom, she will be in." He turned and smiled at her, "Ok see you then." They had gotten so involved with each other they lost all track of time, the lunch rush was going to start and she was needed at the deli. "I have never been late for work; you are a bad influence on me, Mr. Naples." She told him teasingly. "I don't care I would do it again …..If we had time." they smiled at each other and left for the deli.

Connie and Dom knew Sam and Nick had gotten closer, but never imagined how close. Sam was radiant and he could not stop smiling, Dom pulled him aside," Little brother, you better not hurt this girl she is like a daughter to me." Nick put his hand on Dom's shoulder, "Big brother, why would I hurt the most wonderful woman in the world? I love her and hope to make a life with her." Dom was pleased and hurried out back to tell Connie. His beautiful wife was sitting down resting for a moment, her belly was getting bigger and she was not a large woman so she tired easily. "He said he loves Sam!" she was so excited she squealed with joy. Sam came running to her to see what was wrong; Connie put her arms out to Sam and hugged her, "I am so happy for you and Nick." "Well, I guess the secret is out isn't it?" she beamed and went back to work

— CHAPTER 7 —

The next five months were full of meetings and decisions about the design house. Nick and Sam spent free every minute together, talking, planning and making love every chance they could. The building was coming together beautifully, he thought of every detail to make Sam's dream come true. The time to open the doors was about 3 weeks away and Nick was making plans for the grand opening when he got a call from Dom, "Nicholas, It's time for the baby, meet us at the hospital." Dom was so excited he forgot to tell him what hospital before he hung up. Nick called Sam, "Sam, it's time to go to the hospital but I don't know which one." Sam giggled, "I know which one, come pick me up we can go together." He didn't know his way around, he was so thankful Sam did.

They arrived at the hospital just in time to see Connie going into the operating room. Dom was right next to her dressed like a surgeon; he spotted them, whispered something to his wife and came to greet them.

"It's time; I am going to be a father! I'm so glad you are both here." Then he hurried away to be with Connie. Samantha and Nick found the waiting room, they sat together holding hands and talking about how exciting this all was and how happy they were for Connie and Dom. Hours had passed and still no word, just when Nick was going to ask a nurse to check on them a Doctor came out of the room, "Excuse me, but could you tell me how my sister-in-law Constance Naples is doing?" He turned to Nick and took his mask off his face, Sam was stunned; it was David, the one man she hoped to never see again. He talked to

Nick for just a moment and walked away. "The doctor says it will be any time now and they are all fine. Sam, are you alright?" Sam just shook all over, "Sam, what's wrong?"

Sam looked at him as if a ghost just passed by. "I have to leave, NOW!" She jumped up and ran out of the hospital; he chased her to the car. "Sam what is going on?" She could not tell him, not right now, not on the day when they should be so happy. Sam put her head on his chest and cried, "Baby what is it?" "Oh, Nick I can't talk about it right now, maybe later, please be patient with me." He held her tightly and kissed her forehead to reassure her he was there for her. She clung to him so close he knew something was definitely wrong, but what could it be to upset her so badly? After she calmed down he talked her into going back in with him, but she was hesitant and he knew it so he stayed as close to her as he could.

They had just resumed their places back in the waiting room when Dominic came running out to them, "It's a girl! I have a daughter!" Nick jumped up and hugged his brother, "Congratulations, that's wonderful, how is Connie?" "She's wonderful but exhausted, can you believe it, a little girl" Sam stood next to Dom trying to be excited for them but could not shake the thought of David. "I am so happy for you both" She hugged him and sat back in her chair. The two brothers talked for a few more minutes and Dom went back to his wife and child. Nick came to Sam and helped her up, "Let's go home and get some sleep, we can come back in the morning." Sam held on to him like she would fall if she let go, he was so concerned his heart ached for her.

They did not speak all the way home, when they got into the apartment Sam ran to the bathroom, she was feeling sick to her stomach, Nick made some tea and waited for her to come out. After what seemed like a lifetime she finally came into the kitchen and sat down. He gave her a cup of tea and sat with her, "If you don't want to talk I understand but Sam you are a wreck and I love you so much it is killing me to see you like this." She took her cup and went into the living room to the couch, where they had made love so many times. It was a comfortable place for her, feeling the love they had was the only thing keeping her together right now.

"I need to tell you something but it is so hard to talk about and it may take a while." "Baby, you can tell me anything and take all the time you need, I am not going anywhere." She could not look at him while she told him; she was so embarrassed about the whole thing. She started to tell him all the nasty, mean things an old boyfriend had done to her, constant put downs and criticism, judging everything she did and said. Then the fighting and beatings she took from this man and finally the rape she had endured from him. Nick listened without trying to say anything or stop her even though it was tearing him apart to hear this. When she was done telling him the past, she told him about what happened in the hospital, he wanted to go back there and confront this man he was so angry that someone would do this to his Sam. "I'm sorry I didn't tell you this before but I never thought it would make a difference in our life, I never thought I would ever see him again. Forgive me?"

He pulled her close to him, "There is nothing to forgive, you can tell me anything about your past that would not make me love you any less, you are my world now, I am only sorry I didn't know you then." Sam snuggled up to him and inhaled his scent, "I'm here now and you have nothing to fear from that man any more." She felt so safe with him, so loved it almost made her forget her past. She fell asleep in his arms and he gently lifted her up and put her into their bed, he quietly closed the door and sat in the darkness of the living room, drinking tea and trying to understand all that he had heard tonight.

— CHAPTER 8 —

Dom went to the deli and hung a sign on the door, "CLOSED TODAY, WE HAD A GIRL! He hurried to the hospital to be with his family, arms full of flowers and gifts for them. "Good morning my beautiful wife, how is the most wonderful woman in the world." Connie smiled, "I am feeling a little tired but I am so happy I don't want to sleep. Did you stop and see her in the nursery, isn't she the most beautiful baby you have ever seen?" He shook his head with tears in his eyes and kissed her, "I love you. Has the doctor been in to see you this morning?" "Yes, he says everything is fine and he would see me in 3 weeks at his office. Our baby needs a name Dom, what are we going to call her?" He sat and thought about it for a while, "How about Grace?" Connie looked at him and smiled, "Yes I love it, and Grace is a perfect name for her."

They called in the nurse and filled out all the papers that were needed for Grace to be named. The nurse took the papers, "Would you like me to bring Grace in to see you now?" Dominic beamed, "Yes please, I would like to hold my daughter." The nurse was soon back with a small bundle in a pink blanket, "Here she is, all bathed and ready for her Mommy and Daddy." Connie took the child in her arms, with tears in her eyes, "Hello my beautiful girl, I am your mommy and that handsome man over there is your daddy." She gently kissed her and handed her to Dom. He was so nervous he had beads of sweat on his forehead, his wife giggled at him, "She is a blessing isn't she." He nodded and stared at his daughter wiggling in his arms.

The nurse opened the door," Are you ready for visitors?" Connie nodded, in walked Nick and Samantha the two people who meant the world to them. They all hugged and chatted for a minute, "Nick would you like to hold your godchild?" Dom brought Grace to him. He held her close to his chest and kissed her forehead, "My heart is racing, she is beautiful, hello baby girl I am your Uncle Nick." He rocked her and whispered to her about what a glorious life she will have and how he would always be there for her. Sam watched him with a smile on her face, so touched by the gentleness of this man she loved so much.

Nick brought Grace to Sam, "And this is your Aunt Sam, isn't she beautiful, you two will be great friends" She held Grace for a while longer just watching her in amazement then gave her to her mother. "She is a gift." Sam stepped back to the window, trying to hide her fear of running into David again.

Nick touched her shoulder, "We should go, and we have a busy day ahead of us." She agreed and they said their good-byes. Standing in front of the elevator, Sam got a cold feeling in the pit of her stomach; she looked around and saw him, David. He spotted her, "Samantha, is that you?" she froze with fear. Nick held her next to him like a protective father. "What a small world, what are you doing here?" Sam looked at the face that has put so much pain in her life, "My best friend just had a baby." He nodded his head, "I thought I saw you last night in the waiting room. You mean Connie Naples?" She nodded; Nick held the elevator door, "Come on Sam we have to go."

She got in the elevator and clung to him. When the doors closed she broke down, he held her close till the doors opened and he took her to the car. They sat for a bit in silence till she could compose herself, "I'm sorry, it just brings it all back seeing him." Nick was silent, "Will it ever go away, this fear?" He turned to her," Yes my love it will, I promise." The day proceeded as planned, with only a slight shadow of the morning events. Nick handled all the arrangements for the opening and Sam ordered all her supplies and began interviewing people to work for them. At the end of the day they both sat in her office area just looking at the progress they had made. He turned away from her, fumbling around in his pocket, "I have one more thing to take care of" he turned to her with a very stern look on his face, "Samantha Trent, if you marry me I promise never to hurt you or make you cry, I will love you forever."

Sam stopped writing, stared at him in disbelief with tears in her eyes, "Nick are you sure? You really want to get married, to me" He smiled that smile that she loved so much, "With all my heart." He opened the box in his hand; it was the most beautiful heart shaped diamond she had ever seen. He took it out of the box and put it on her finger, it fit perfect just like she did in his life. Sam was overwhelmed, "Yes, Nick I will marry you, I love you." She leaned into his face and kissed him with every bit of love and passion she felt the first time she kissed his lips. "If you keep that up we will never get out of here, I will have to have you right here." She stood up and dropped her dress to the floor, "I am yours, take me." He made love to her like it was the first time, exploring her body like he had never seen it before. She moaned at his every touch, wanting him more than ever. When he entered her she arched to him so passionately he was out of control with arousal, but remained gentle with her. He loved her repeatedly, till he was so worn out from the excitement, he had to stop. Sam ran her fingers down his chest as he lay next to her on the floor, "I am so in love with you Nick." She kissed his neck, he moaned," No more baby, I am wiped out." He smiled at her with a gleam in her eye, she grinned, "I guess we better get dressed and get to Dom's house, they will be waiting for us. So do they know about this?" "I hope not, I never expected to be making love on your office floor."

She smirked at him holding up her hand, "Oh, you mean the ring; no I didn't want to tell them till you said yes." "Did you think I would say no?" He laughed, "There is always that possibility." They laughed, got dressed and went on their way. All the way to Dom's, Sam kept looking at her ring and looking at him, this can't be a dream and if it is May I never wake up.

The house was all lit up, people were coming to see the baby and with Dom and Connie all their best. Nick and Sam walked in the front door and were immediately spotted by Dom, "Hey, you two where have you been, we have been waiting for you" He crossed the room to them and handed them both a glass of wine. "Everybody, I wish to make a little speech, please indulge me for a bit. On this the happiest day of our lives I want to thank you all for coming and joining in our celebration. Our prayers have been answered, Grace is our blessing, and may she know all the love, security and friendship that we do. We could never ask for more support and friendship than we have here today. I have one more thing to say before I let you all go back to your conversations. My brother; Nicholas has consented to be godfather for our baby, now we need to know if Samantha will be her godmother. Sam, would you?" Sam didn't know what to say, she took one look at Grace in her bassinet, "Of course, I would be honored." everyone applauded and congratulated her. As she hugged Dom, Connie screamed, "Oh my god, Sam, are you engaged?"

Grabbing her hand and staring at her newly acquired ring. Sam and Nick beamed at each other, "Why yes we are, is that ok with you and Dom?" Dom grabbed his brother with so much joy he was ready to bust. Connie wrapped her arms around Sam, "I am so happy for you Sam." Everyone there was so happy for them, even baby Grace was smiling at her new Aunt and Uncle.

As the night wore on people began to leave but not without giving best wishes to both couples. It was one of the most joyous nights Sam ever had. After the last guest had left Sam and Connie started to clean up while Dom and Nick took Grace to her nursery. "They are so wonderful with her, she already adores them both. Little do they know she will have them wrapped around her finger before she is 2 months old." They both laughed, "She already has her daddy jumping every time she whimpers." Sam watched Nick go up the stairs holding Grace with such a gentleness her heart swelled. "He will be a wonderful father too." Connie broke in, Sam smiled, "I think so too." While the two of them finished up the dishes, the men walked outside to the gazebo, sharing their joy and discussing future plans. "May we join you gentlemen?" Sam glanced at Nick with a grin. "Of course, my love come sit with me." Connie joined Dom on the swing, snuggling like newlyweds. "This has been such a great night I hate to see it end, but we do have to get some sleep, we have so much to do in the next few months. Not to mention you two have a little bundle up stairs that will be waking you up pretty early." They all agreed, Connie was exhausted from all the excitement so Dom helped her in the house and they said their good-byes.

Nick walked Sam to the car, he could not wait another moment, and he spun her around and kissed her welcoming mouth. "Now we can go home and you may have your way with me" he whispered. She smiled at him with anticipation. He kissed her again and helped her in to the car. The drive home felt like it took forever, Sam was so anxious to be with him, to feel his body next to hers and to give herself to him again.

— CHAPTER 9 —

The apartment was a welcome sight to them after a very emotional and long day. They took a long hot shower and fell into bed. She nuzzled his neck and ran her fingers up his leg, he tried to lay still but she could see he was aroused. He wanted her, he tried to hold back but his passion over took him and she was his, body and soul. She had never been so willing to give herself to anyone, but he was so gentle, so passionate when they made love she could not refuse him anything no matter how many times he asked. Their lovemaking went on till the wee hours and Sam finally fell asleep in his arms. He listened to her breath and felt her heart beat against him, "Thank you god for this woman."

The deli was busier than ever, people were coming in to congratulate Dom and ask about the baby. Sam and Dom worked alone so Connie could stay at home with the baby for a few weeks.

Her mother was coming to stay with them to help out with the baby, but she would not be here for at least a week. After the customers had all gone Sam and Dom sat at the counter, had some ice tea and talked. "So have you and Nick set a date?" "Not yet, we want to wait till after the grand opening is over and see what happens from there." He nodded his head, "I hope you two don't wait to long. I want a niece or nephew to spoil too." Sam was surprised that he would say something like that to her he had always been so fatherly with her. "You look surprised Sam, well don't be, you are now officially family and I can speak my mind to you, so I guess you better get used to it."

He smiled and went into the back room to cook for the next day. Sam cleaned the tables and counter from the lunch crowd, all the while thinking about Nick. Smiling to herself she walked behind the counter and heard someone come in the door. Hoping it would be Nick; she looked out and was shocked at who she saw. David, he was there, she panicked at the sight of him. "Hello Samantha I finally tracked you down." Sam stood perfectly still, "Are you surprised to see me? I guess you never thought I would walk in here huh?" She looked out back, "Dom would you come out here please?" Dom walked out, "Hey Doc what are you doing here?" David look disappointed, "Well I came to look up an old friend." He gestured toward Sam, "Do you work here too?" "Hell, I own the place. Can I get you anything?" "No thanks I just wanted to talk to Samantha." "Well good to see you Doc, stop by again sometime I have work to do."

He went back into the kitchen area leaving Sam alone with her nightmare. "I wondered if we could get together sometime and talk." He approached her slowly, Sam looked at him in amazement, "Have you got nerve, coming here and asking me to spend time with you. I told you I never wanted to see you ever again and I meant it." He frowned, "But Sam, we were just kids then, I would like to think we have grown past all that. Besides who knew you would turn out to be such a beauty?" he reached out to touch her cheek. Just then Sam heard a voice from the back room, "I don't think you need to be here sir and I know Sam wants you to leave." It was Nick; he walked over to Sam and put his arm around her, "Right Baby." Sam nodded in agreement; David started to act uneasy. "I just wanted to get together with an old friend."

Sam glared at him, "You are no friend of mine David, old or new now please leave and don't try to contact me again!" "You heard the lady now leave." Nick took his arm showed him to the door as he slowly walked through it, he turned around to Sam, "Nice seeing you again Samantha" Nick slammed the door in his face and watched to make sure he was gone. Sam fell into a chair shaking; Nick went to her and held her, till she was steady enough to stand on her own.

Dom came out, "Hey I didn't know you knew the Doc, great guy isn't he?" Nick looked at Sam, "You have to tell him Nick, He should know what kind of man his wife has for a doctor." He agreed and went to Dom, "Big brother we have to talk." They went into the back room and Nick told him what Sam said to him the other night, Dom came out to Sam, "I am so sorry Sam, I didn't know, Connie will find another

doctor right away, I don't want him touching my wife or my daughter."
He hugged her like a father, kissed her forehead and went back to work.
Nick sat with her to make sure she was alright, "Sam do you think you
should talk to someone about this, a professional?" She thought about
it for a minute, "No I have dealt with it all these years without anyone's
help I think now that I have you I will be just fine." She kissed him,
got up steadying herself and finishes her work. He watched her closely
to make sure she was fine, he would die if anything happened to her,
he waited so long to find a woman like her and he was not going to
let anyone hurt her. When Sam was done cleaning up she got her self
together and said good night to Dom. "See you in the morning, Dom."
He waved to them and they walked out to the car, "I feel like walking
if you don't mind, the fresh air will help me clear my head ok?" Nick
agreed and took her hand, "Whatever my baby wants."

She smiled at him and they walked in silence. By the time they got
to her apartment she was feeling much better, she knew Nick would
always be there for her, it put her mind at ease.

There was a knock at the door, Sam jumped, and Nick answered the
door. "Yes" "I have a special delivery letter for Miss Samantha Trent."
"I'll sign for her" he tipped the boy and brought the envelope to Sam.
"For you baby, should I be worried?" Sam smiled and opened the letter;
it was from her father's attorney, "It's a copy of Daddy's will, I forgot all
about this." She quickly opened it and began reading, "It says I inherited
half of everything from my father. He enclosed a check for my half;
he says Stephen and Victoria sold everything including the house." She
opened the envelope with the check in it, "Nicholas! Oh my goodness,
I have never seen so many numbers on one check." Nick looked at it,
"Well, I guess you never have to work again." She giggled, "I will work
until I can't anymore this will go into our future."

He was impressed, most women would take the money and run,
not his Sam she is so practical and level headed. "What ever you want
to do with it Sam is up to you, you know I make very good money,
more than enough to support a very nice lifestyle." "I know but I want
to use this for exactly what my father wanted for me, he wanted me to
find my one true love and hang on for dear life and that is exactly what
I am doing, so this is for us." She put all the papers away and the check
went in her purse to go to the bank in the morning, got her robe out

and went to shower, to wash off the feeling of David that was left on her. When she came out into the living room Nick had set up a candle light dinner for two, he stood by the table with her chair pulled out, "Your dinner is served my love." She sat at the table looking at all he had done for her, "You are full of surprises aren't you?" he just grinned, "Wait till you see what's for dessert." The dinner was wonderful and his company was just what she needed. Afterwards she sat on the couch and watched him while he cleaned up the table. When he was finished he came to her with a single red rose, "Are you ready for dessert?" She smiled and took his hand following him to the bedroom; he lit candles and put on some soft music.

"Nick, I don't want to wait to get married, can we set a date now?" He was surprised at how eager she was to get married, "Well when would you like to get married?" She sat and thought about it, "How about next week before Grace is christened." He was overjoyed, "If you're sure, then we will." Sam beamed at him, "I have never been more sure of anything in my life." With that decision made they embraced their love and fell asleep in each others arms.

The morning was full of excitement for Sam, she told Dom about their plans to wed next week, he was so happy for her. "We will make all the food for you and we can have a reception at our house, hell you can have the ceremony there too!" Sam liked that idea, "Let me talk to Nick, but I know he will agree." "Will agree about what?" Nick asked as he walked in the back room. She told him Dom's idea and he was very touched by what his brother offered. "Sam have you thought about who we will invite? Any of your family?" Sam frowned, "No one I would invite except Margie." Nick was surprised, but knew she meant it, "Ok Margie will be invited, and I will invite the rest of my family, there aren't a lot of them left but I would love for them to be here." Sam smiled, "I think that's a wonderful gesture, Darling, I can't wait to meet them all." She kissed him and went to work.

The rest of the day was busy deciding all the final details for the wedding. Sam knew exactly what design she was going to make for her dress, it was something she had done years ago but it was a classic style and she knew it would be perfect for their special day. Being very petite, she knew it would not take much fabric or much time to make it. They called an old friend of Dom's, a judge who was a regular customer at the deli and he was honored to be asked to perform the ceremony. "Flowers, food, location and the judge, I guess we are pretty well set." Nick smiled at Sam and Dom, "Connie will be so excited when I tell her, she loves you two so much, and she will feel like the mother of the bride and the groom!" They all laughed at the joke but they also knew it was true.

As the week went on Sam and Nick finalized the plans for the grand opening of the design house, it would be the week after they returned from their honeymoon. He was brought some of his best people out from California to set everything up in the building; he wanted it perfect for her. They had hired the staff and gotten only the best fabrics and notions, he had things shipped in from all over the world.

Sam had never seen such a production before, she was overwhelmed by it all and even a little scared. "Nick this is so much to handle right now, do you think we should wait to get married, until after the opening?" Nick stopped dead, "Are you saying you don't want to get married?" She shook her head, "No, but I am just trying to make things a little easier on you. Between the wedding and the opening I am afraid you are over run with it all." He grinned at her, "Don't you worry about me I am used to this kind of pace. I do have another design house remember?" "Yes, but it just seems like so much work and I am not much help to you other than picking fabrics and notions." "You and your designs are the reason I am doing all of this, believe me when we get back from our honeymoon you will be doing all the work and I will be able to relax." He had made all the plans for the honeymoon, the design house and most of the wedding plans, he loved every minute of it too.

"By the way Sam, I have to go to California, I am leaving in the morning and I promise I will be back in more than enough time for the wedding." Sam felt a rush of fear come over her, was he running out on her, maybe he finally decided it was to much to be with her, she did not say a word to him, "Baby, did you hear me?" She shook her head, "Yes I heard you, are you sure you are coming back or is this your way of telling me good-bye?" "WHAT! Have you lost your mind? I have to tie up some lose ends out there before the wedding, that's all, I am coming back and you will be my wife this Saturday. My god Sam, have I not proven to you how much you mean to me yet?" She started to cry, "I'm sorry, it is all so much like a dream I guess I am just waiting for it to blow up in my face. Dreams do end you know, at least in my life they do." He put his arms around her waist, kissed her neck, "You are amazing Samantha Trent, this dream will never end not as long as I am alive. Just call me your 'Sandman'." Her body automatically moved into his, like it had so many times, being in his arms was all she needed to forget her crazy thoughts about him leaving her. "I love you Nicholas Naples." "I love you too Mrs. Naples" Sam loved the sound of that so much she wrapped her arms around his neck and kissed him.

A knock on the door interrupted them, "Yes?" In walked Jan, Nick's secretary form California, "Hello Sir, I just wanted to stop by and see what we are working with before the rest of the staff arrives; it is a beautiful building indeed." Sam approached her, "Hi, I am Samantha Trent; it is so nice to meet you, Jan." They shook hands and Nick picked up some papers and handed them to Jan, "These are the contracts we discussed, please go over them as usual. We can get together later to make sure we have everything covered." Jan nodded, "Yes Sir, it was a pleasure to meet you Miss Trent, I look forward to working with you, the boss says you have talent like no one he has ever seen." "Thank you." Sam smiled at the woman as she left the office. "Wow, you must have a hell of a staff out there if she is any example." He smiled, "I have been very lucky with my staff, they are the best." It was getting late and they had finished all they could for one day, "Ready to go Sam?" They packed up all their papers and locked the doors, standing outside the building Sam looked up at the brightly lit sign, "Naples House of Design" it was the most beautiful thing she had ever seen.

— CHAPTER 10 —

Sam made dinner while Nicholas packed for his trip; this was the first time they would be separated since he returned all those months ago. Sam was saddened to think about not seeing him even for a couple days, "Sam? Has Dom found someone to replace you at the deli yet?" She had forgotten about the deli, who was Dom going to replace her with. In less than a week she would never be working at the deli again and Dom really depended on her. "I don't know, he hasn't said anything about it."

It was going to be sad to leave the deli, never to work with Dom and Connie again but Sam knew what she was doing was for the best. She was fulfilling her dreams and more. Nick's bags were packed and by the door, "All packed and ready to go, my flight leaves at 5 am so I will take a cab to the airport so you can get some rest. You will be so busy while I am gone you won't even miss me." He hugged Sam, "I will think of you every second and you know it." They sat silently through dinner, both distracted by what they had to do for the next few days.

She heard the cab's horn and jumped out of bed, he was already out the door. She ran to the window, swung it open, "Nick, I love you, hurry back." He turned around and looked up to her hanging out the window, "I love you baby see you in a couple of days." She stood there watching the cab pull away feeling sick to her stomach. When she could no longer see the tail lights she ran to the bathroom and threw-up. Well this was strange, maybe I am more upset than I thought, she made herself some tea and crackers to settle her stomach and sat at the table reading the papers she brought home from the office. She worked on them for hours, the phone broke her concentration, "Nick?"

"Hello Miss Sam, its Margie. Are you alright?" "Yes Margie I was just waiting for Nick to call. How are you?" "I am well, Miss Sam, I just wanted to call to let you know I am here at the hotel. I am so happy you wanted me here for your wedding. Is there anything I can do to help you?" "No thank you Margie I just want you to be here, you have always had a special place in my heart and it means the world to me that you came." "I wouldn't miss it." They talked awhile longer and Sam invited Margie to meet her at the deli for lunch, she agreed. Sam was so pleased she knew she would never miss the happiest day of her life. She got ready and went to the deli; she had time before Margie was to arrive so she went out back and talked to Dom. "Dom have you found someone to replace me yet?" He turned to her, "I haven't found anyone yet Sam, but don't worry you have a life with Nick now and this place will be fine."

She half smiled at him, "But Dom, I really can't leave till I know you have someone to work with." "You have your design house and your wedding coming up, that should be the least of your worries, besides I have two people coming for interviews today after lunch." She was relieved to hear that, just then she heard the font door, she went out to find Margie standing at the counter. The two women hugged each other; it had been a long time since Margie was able to hug Sam like that. "Miss Sam, you look radiant, it must be Mr. Nick putting that glow on your face. Where is your man, I am so anxious to meet him?" She looked around the deli, "He is away on business but he will be back in a couple days, you will meet him then." Dom came out to see what was going on; he was feeling very protective of Sam now that he knew about David. "Hello, I'm Dominic" and he shook Margie's hand, "It's a pleasure to me you Mr. Dominic" "Just call me Dom, we are practically family now right?" Margie smiled at him, "Thank you Mr. Dom." Sam was so pleased that Margie finally met Dom, she wrote to her about Dom and Connie but it just means so much to have them meet. "Would you like something to drink or eat Margie?"

Dom asked and without waiting for an answer he went and got her a plate of food and a tall iced tea. He set it on the table for her and went back to the kitchen area to give them some privacy. They talked about everything that has happened since Sam got back, Margie was amazed at it all. "Miss Sam you look so happy, it does my heart good to see you like this. You know after Mr. Stephen sold the house I had to go live in a motel for a bit, seems no one wants an aging housekeeper." Sam was saddened to think of Margie struggling, then she had a thought, "Hang on a minute, I need to talk to Dom for a bit." And off she went, when she returned Dom was with her, both smiling at Margie.

"What is wrong, Miss Sam?" "Nothing, Dom and I have an idea." As Samantha talked Margie could not believe what she was hearing, "Me, here?" "Yes you here. You could work for Dom and Connie and live in my apartment, Nick and I will be getting a house soon so it would all be yours. What do you think?" Margie thought about it for a bit, "Ok, I'll do it. You are my family now right? So I should be near my family." They all laughed, "That's right Margie, and you should be near family." Dom repeated. Margie ate and drank till she could not hold another bite, the food was delicious, "Mr. Dom this food is the best I have ever had, no wonder you are so busy in here all the time." He smiled at her compliment, he knew she would work out in the deli, just as well as Sam did. Sam invited Margie to go to the design house with her; she wanted her to see all that Nick had done. They took a cab to the building, Margie could not believe the size of it, "Miss Sam it is enormous!" Sam laughed, "Wait till you see inside." The two women entered the building, people were all over doing all the last minute touches for the opening, Jan greeted them at the door, "Hello, Miss Trent" "Sam please, this is my dearest friend in the world, Margie." "Pleasure to meet you Margie; I'm Jan, Mr. Naples and Miss Trent… Sam's secretary." All three women walked around the building while Sam explained what everything was and how a design house works. Jan excused herself to answer a phone call. "Just a moment sir." Jan waved to Sam to come to the phone.

Sam walked to the office, took the phone, "Hello" "How's my baby doing without me?" It was Nick, she beamed just hearing his voice, "I miss you so much already, Nick" They talk about Margie being there and Sam told him about her working for Dom and taking over the apartment when they found a house. "Well, you have been busy; I told you there would be so much for you to do you wouldn't even think about me." "NICHOLAS! How can you think that, you know better?" They both laughed, "Well my love I have to go, my attorneys' are waiting for me, I will call you tonight, I love you baby." "I love you too, bye."

She rejoined her friend and finished out the tour of the building. Margie was so impressed with everything she saw she could not believe one man could do all this by himself. "Your Mr. Nick must be a remarkable man." "He is a dream come true Margie." Margie wanted to tell her that she had received a letter from Mr. Nick with money for her trip and he even paid for her hotel, but he asked her to keep it between them. He just knew that it would make Sam so happy to have her there he had to make sure she was.

After all the excitement of the day Margie was looking very tired, "Are you ok Margie?" "Just a little tired Miss Sam, do you mind if I go back to the hotel and get some rest? We have some busy days coming up and I think I will need all the rest I can get." Sam agreed with her, she haled a cab and dropped Margie off at the hotel, gave the cabby his fee and decided to walk home it was only a few blocks from the hotel. As she walked down the fairly quiet street, she could hear someone walking behind her. The footsteps quickened as hers did, she started to get nervous, who was this following her?

She felt her heart racing as she tried to find a store front to go into, but it was late and they were all closed. Sam was walking so fast she was almost running and the footsteps behind her were keeping up with her. She turned a corner, one block from her apartment, when she felt a hand on her shoulder pulling her back.

She tried to scream but the gloved hand over her mouth stopped her. "Well, if it isn't my old friend Samantha." When she heard David's voice she froze, "I knew when I saw Margie leaving the hotel she was going to meet you, my patience paid off, I finally got you alone." Sam listened to him, praying for the strength to get away. She was such a small woman and he was a big man, so much stronger than her.

He pulled her up against him and started pulling at her clothes. Suddenly, she felt a hard tug on her shoulder, someone had pulled him off her and she turned around to see it was Dom, where did he come from, how did he know? Dom beat David to the ground, repeatedly punching him till David curled up and begged him to stop. "Dominic, stop!" Sam screamed, he backed away from the beaten mass on the sidewalk, "Get up you scum!" David got up slowly, blood all over his face and head, "Get out of here and don't ever let me catch you around her again!"

After he ran off, Dom grabbed Sam, "Are you ok little one?" Sam sobbed in his chest. "How did you know?" Dom held her tightly, "I was at the hotel making final arrangements for the wedding guests and when I came out I saw him following you and I knew he was up to no good." Sam was so grateful to him, he walked her to her apartment, took her inside and made sure all the doors and windows were locked and she was safe, "If you need me again you call me I don't care what time it is, you understand me Samantha." He was stern like a father; Sam agreed and hugged him in gratitude, "What would I have done without you Dom." He kissed her forehead, "You are my family now Sam." and left.

Sam clicked the button on her answering machine, five messages, all from Nick, he sounded panicked wondering where she was, like he knew something was wrong. Sam called him, "Hi darling it's me." "Sam? Where have you been I have been so worried, I thought you would be home long before now?" She decided not to tell him about David, not right now he would do nothing but worry, and it could wait. Besides, Dom took care of it, thank god for that man. "I took Margie back to her hotel and walked home from there, it was a beautiful night and the walk did me good, I'm fine" Nick knew she was lying, something was wrong he could feel it.

"Baby are you sure you're ok?" "Yes, I'm fine, home safe and sound. Stop worrying, it will make you old before your time." Nick still felt uneasy but decided to let it go till he got back, nothing he could do from California anyway. "Ok Sam if you say so, did you have a good day with Margie?" Sam tried to talk to him about the whole day, but she was so exhausted from it all she couldn't. He could hear how tired she was, "Sam go get some sleep, and I will call you in the morning ok? I love you baby." "Ok, I love you too. Good night."

Nick was sure something had happened and she was not going to tell him so he called his brother to see if he knew what was going on. When Dom answered the phone he sounded very agitated, "Hey Dom its Nick, everything ok?" Dom was hesitant to tell him what had happened, he would go crazy worrying. "Dom are you alright?"

"Yeah Nick I am, are you doing ok, getting everything taken care of out there?" "Dom, something's wrong, what is it, is Connie alright? Grace?" "Yes, yes they are both fine, Nick don't worry we are all fine. When are you going to be back Nick?" He knew right then it was Sam, "What is it Dom, talk to me" Dom had to tell him, he knew if he didn't he would never forgive him. Dom explained what happened, how he spotted David following Sam and how he stopped him before he could do anything to her. Nick was silent, listening to his brother tell him about what had happened, rage was building inside him, he had been afraid of this since Sam told him about David. "I will kill him when I get back, in fact I am leaving tonight"

Dom knew this would happen, "Nick, please she is fine I took her home and made sure the whole place was locked up and she is safe now. Please don't fly home tonight, I don't think the fine doctor is going to be around to bother her again, I put a pretty good beating on him." Nick smiled at the thought of it, "Dam I wish I could have been there, I'd have loved to beat the hell out of him." The two brothers chuckled about it and made a pact that no matter what that man was never going near any of their family again. When they finally hung up Nicholas went to the window over looking the lake, "Thank you god for Dominic. He saved my life."

— CHAPTER 11 —

Sam woke up early that next morning remembering that Nick would be home tonight, excitement started to build in her just thinking about holding him again. She put on one of his favorite outfits that she designed and went to work. The building was filled with fabric, notions, machines, tables and everything you could think of to manufacture her designs. The show room was decorated so beautifully with satins and silks, couches and chairs and a small runway for private showings. It was all so much more than she had ever imagined and Nick made it all possible. In the midst of all her happiness was a fear that it could've all been taken away in a minute, what if David had gotten away with what he planned, what if he meant to kill her, the fear she felt made her stomach sick. She went into the restroom by her office and vomited; she stood up and looked in the mirror at her pale complexion. "What is wrong with me? Why am I getting sick so much? What if something is really wrong with me?" She left the restroom and went straight to the office, she sat at her desk, dialed the phone and prayed while she listened to it ring. "Hello, Doctor's office." "Hello, this is Samantha Trent; I need an appointment to see the doctor." The nurse was so kind to her, "Ok Miss Trent, we have an opening this afternoon at 2 o'clock is that good for you?" Sam took the appointment, thanked the nurse, hung up and sat in her office till it was time to go.

She walked into the doctor's office, pale and shaking, what if she is really sick, how can she plan a life with Nick if she was sick. After about 15 minutes the nurse called her in, "Hello Miss Trent, what seems to be the problem?" Sam explained what had been happening, the nurse listened and made notes, when Sam was done the nurse handed her a gown, asked her to change and the doctor would be right in. Sam was so scared, all she could think of was Nick and all the plans they had for the future, a future they may not have to share. The doctor came in the room, "Hi Samantha, I see you have been getting sick lately?" Sam nodded, "Well let's check you out and do some blood tests to see what's going on with you." The doctor was gentle and kind and she was very comfortable with him. He finished his exam and had the nurse draw some blood, she gave Sam a cup for a urine sample, "I will be back soon" he said as he left the room.

Sam was so engrossed with her fear of being sick she didn't realize that she had been in there for over 1/2 an hour waiting. Finally, the doctor came in, sat on his stool and smiled at her. "Well, Samantha, we know what's wrong with you." Her eyes grew big and she braced herself for the worst, "Ok, tell me, what is wrong with me." He grinned at her, "Sam you're fine, you're pregnant. About 2 months along. I will need to see you in about a month to check your progress, if you have any questions or problems don't hesitate to call the office." With that he put his hand on her shoulder; "Congratulations." and left the room. Sam sat in amazement, pregnant, I'm pregnant, I'm not sick, I'm pregnant.

The nurse came into see if she was alright, "Miss Trent, are you ok?" Sam beamed at her, "Yes I'm wonderful, I'm pregnant!" the nurse smiled, "Congratulations" Sam got off the exam table and got dressed, she walked out of the office feeling like she was floating on air. She was going to go back to the office but decided to go home instead, the cab dropped her off at her apartment, and she thanked the cabby, gave him a large tip and floated up to her door.

She could not believe it; she was having a baby with the most wonderful man in the world. 'He will be here in a few hours, I better get ready' Sam thought to herself. She showered, put on something comfortable and went in to the kitchen to make a very special dinner for Nick. She set up a candle lit dinner, soft music and all his favorite foods; she wanted this to be a night he would never forget. When everything was set she stretched out on the couch to rest for a bit, she fell asleep and never even heard him walk in the door.

She felt a warm, familiar kiss on her lips; she opened her eyes to see the man she loved so very much was home. She wrapped her arms around him so tight she never wanted to let go. "Hello, baby, I'm home, miss me?" She was so excited to see him she couldn't talk all she could do was hug and kiss him. "I guess you did" he said jokingly. He stood next to the couch, "I see dinner is ready, it looks beautiful shall we eat or did you have something else in mind" grinning at her. "Nicholas, I hope you never lose your desire for me." He snuggled in to her neck, "Not likely my love."

She pulled away from him and lead him into the kitchen, "I am starved aren't you, after your trip you must be hungry" Nick looked at her with a pouting face, "I guess we can eat first." They laughed, sat down and he began to tell her all about his trip, the attorneys, the paper work and the lonely nights without her. They finished dinner, took coffee into the living room, he wanted to talk to her about what had happened with David but he did not want to upset her, she was in such a good mood, he had never seen her so lit up before.

"What's going on Sam, you look like you are about to bust." Sam climbed on his lap, "Nick I have something to tell you" he watched her closely waiting for her to tell him what Dom had already told him. He listened to her tell him about being sick and going to the doctor. His face went pale thinking the worst, and then she smiled at him, "We are having a baby!" He was numb, "A what?" Sam yelled, "A BABY!" He could not believe his ears; this woman he loves more than his own life is carrying his child. He picked her up and squeezed her to him, he pulled away far enough to see her face, and she had tears running down her cheeks. "Did I hurt you? Oh Sam I'm sorry I didn't mean to, I'm just so happy." Sam smiled at him "No you didn't hurt me I'm so happy I can't control my tears." Nick wanted to ask her all kinds of questions but she looked so beautiful he picked her up, kissed her and took her to bed. They made love passionately; he had missed her so much. When they were satisfied she snuggled up to him, kissed him and fell fast asleep. He couldn't sleep he was so excited about the baby; all he could do was lay there and smile while he listened to her breath. He gently put his hand on her stomach, "You will never know fear, I promise." Sam moaned a little and snuggled in closer to him; he held her and finally went to sleep.

That morning was the day before the wedding, Sam was glowing, she was so full of love for Nick and now for the baby too. They quickly grabbed some breakfast and went to the office. Jan greeted them at the door and brought Nick up to date on the contracts and all the work that had been done. He was pleased with what he was hearing, Jan was very efficient and Nick knew if she was handling things they were done the way he wanted. Sam walked around with him and talked about her ideas and how much she loved the showroom. Nick knew this was a good idea from the start, he just never expected all the love between them to be as good as it was.

Jan went to the door to greet someone, it was Connie and Grace, and they walked in to the showroom where Sam and Nick were. "Sam are you ok?" Connie looked concerned. Sam looked scared, she had not told Nick about David and was hoping Connie would not let it out, not right now. Sam quickly made an excuse to leave the room; she took Connie and Grace to the office, "I have not told Nick about that night, I will, just not today." Connie seemed puzzled, "But Nick talked to Dom and he told him all about it."

Sam fell back in the chair in disbelief, "He knows?" She could not understand why he never said anything, "He never told me, but with everything that has been going on I guess I know why." She wanted so bad to tell her about the baby but they agreed to wait to tell anyone till after the wedding. Grace was sleeping so peacefully in her mother's arms; Sam couldn't wait to hold her baby. Nick came up to the office, "Girl talk or can anyone join in?" They both smiled and welcomed him in. He walked over to Grace and kissed her gently on the forehead, she didn't even stir. "She is so beautiful just like her mommy." Nick was so proud of his brother's family; it made him think of his own soon to be family, he turned to Sam and smiled adoringly. After talking to Connie to make sure everything was set for the wedding Sam was getting hungry, "Could we go to the deli for lunch, I'm hungry?" Nick agreed and escorted all three ladies out to the car.

They walked in the deli just as the lunch rush was ending, Margie greeted them and Dom came out from the back to kiss his wife and daughter. Margie was doing well her first day, Dom was pleased with her. He introduced her to Connie and Grace; Sam sat down with Nick, waiting till they were done talking. Margie came over to their table, "So this is Mr. Nicholas, it is such a pleasure to finally meet you sir." She shook his hand and winked at Sam with approval. "Please call me Nick;

you are family to Sam that makes you family to me too." She smiled very pleased and went back to work. Dom and Connie came over to sit with them, Dom brought them food, and Sam was starving so she just dove right in.

"Sorry I guess I need to feed her more" Nick joked. Dom had some cooking to do so he excused himself and went to the kitchen, "He is such a hard working man, and I can't imagine my life without him."

Connie said admiring her husband as he walked away. "We are the luckiest women in the world, right Sam?" She nodded, still chewing her food, never missing a beat. Sam finally finished, "I am so full but it was so good, thank you." Nick was amazed that such a little woman could eat so much; he leaned over to her, whispering, "Better be careful, our secret will be out." She smiled and kissed him on the cheek, "not a chance of that yet, they probably figure you had your way with me last night." They both giggled.

Dom came out as they were getting ready to leave, "Hey little brother you better plan on staying with us tonight, and you can't see the bride before the wedding." Nick acted like a disappointed child, "But I don't want to be away from her again." Margie spoke up "I will stay with Miss Sam tonight, she will not be alone." Dom smiled, "There, now you have to stay at my house, there will be no room for you at Sam's" Sam giggled and Nick agreed, "I will be at your house before midnight, I promise." Dom nodded in agreement and went back to work.

They left the deli full and happy; Nick decided that if he had to leave her tonight he was going to be with her before he left. He drove past the office and straight to the apartment, he hurried her up the stairs and in the door, like someone was chasing them. He swept her up in his arms and took her to the bed; she was giggling the whole way. "Nicholas what has gotten in to you?" He grinned and took his clothes off, she looked at him admiring his body, his muscles rippled with every movement, he jumped in the bed next to her, "Well aren't you going to take off your clothes?" She eagerly complied with his wishes.

He kissed her gently on the neck; she moaned at his touch, they made love for hours, making up for being apart. He lay next to her holding her close, "Nick, why didn't you tell me you talked to Dom the other night?" He didn't speak, she looked at him and he had tears in his eyes, "Nick, what is it?" He wiped his eyes, "I was so thankful

Dominic was there for you but it should have been me, I promise I will never leave you like that again." He hugged her, "When I think of what could have happened to you, Sam, I want to kill that man."

Sam was so thankful he was not upset with her she kissed him, "I am fine, and yes thank god Dom was there, but it's over and you have nothing to feel bad about and as far as David is concerned I heard his reputation here is ruined, to many people heard about what he tried to do to me. He is moving out west so we never have to deal with him again." Nick was relieved to hear that, "I will never let anything happen to you or our baby ever again." Sam lay next to him, content and happy, "I know, we love you too. But I think you better leave, Margie will be here any minute and you have to go to Dom's." He slowly got out of bed, got dressed and kissed her good bye "I will see you at the altar."

— CHAPTER 12 —

The wedding day was sunny with just enough breeze to keep everyone comfortable. The yard was decorated like a church, flowers everywhere, an arch at the altar and a clothe runner leading to the altar. Connie was scurrying around getting everyone in their right places. The organ started, Nick and Dom stood by the arch waiting for the procession to start, both looking nervous yet handsome in their black tuxedos. Connie came down the aisle first in a blue satin and chiffon dress, her red hair swept up in curls, Dom was so proud of her. Nick was getting antsy waiting to see his Sam, she finally appeared. She was wearing a champagne colored dress, made of satin and chiffon with lace trim at the neck and waist, it was sleeveless with long lace gloves, the train was full but proportioned to her and her head piece was a tiara of diamonds with a modest veil attached. Nick was breathless at the sight of her; she was more radiant than ever. The judge was even impressed by her as she approached he nodded in approval of the beautiful bride. The ceremony was simple but elegant they spoke their vows, both with tears in their eyes. Dom and Connie stood by watching like the proud parents.

When it was all over they kissed so passionately that Dom had to tap them on the shoulders to break it up, all the guests laughed. Sam turned around to Margie, hugged her, "It's even more special with you here my friend." Margie blotted her eyes as the bride and groom walked back down the aisle. The reception following was wonderful, everyone loved the food and were so impressed at all the decorations and the cake Connie made for them; it was seven tiers covered in champagne colored frosting with blue flowers and hearts. Sam and Nick were so involved with each other they barely separated to visit with their guests, but everyone understood and enjoyed the party.

Music, dancing and so much food, it was the event of the season for this small community. People liked Sam and they were impressed with Nick, he was a very sharp businessman. Everyone talked about the up coming opening of the design house, anxious to see Sam's designs. It would put their small town on the map as the home of "Naples House of Design." As the day grew to an end, the guests began to leave; each woman had a piece of cake wrapped in napkins to take home with a crystal bud vase, each man had a crystal goblet engraved with the initials S & N. Connie hired a crew of workers to clean up after the reception; she knew she would be exhausted, while they went to work she and Dom went inside to check on Grace.

Connie's mother had arrived the day before and kept Grace inside during the wedding. She was sound asleep in her crib, "What an angel she is" she whispered. She closed the door and they proceeded to find the newlyweds, when they got downstairs Sam and Nick were standing in the living room, locked in each others arms, "Well here they are, you two make me want to get married all over again." Connie said with a smile. Dom came in with a glass of champagne for each of them, he made a toast to his brother and his new sister-in-law, and they all sipped their drinks except Sam. "You ok Sam? I haven't seen you drink all night." Dom asked concerned. Nick looked at her, "Should we tell them?" Sam smiled at her husband, "The doctor said it wasn't good for me to drink alcohol." Dom walked over to her, with fear in his face, "Sam are you sick? What is it? Can we do anything to help?" Nick smiled at his brother; "Well there is one thing you can do" they both looked at him anxious to help, "You could be Godparents for our baby." Dom and Connie were stunned, they stared at Sam for a moment, "A baby, how wonderful, of course we will be the godparents." Dom was so relieved he about cried. Connie rushed over to Sam and hugged her, "I couldn't be happier for you, both of you." She turned to Nick and hugged him too.

The foursome sat and talked about babies and marriage, laughing at the thought of Nick changing diapers. After about an hour or so Sam was looking tired, "Well, Mrs. Naples, are you ready to go?" She smiled at hearing her new name, "Yes, Mr. Naples I am." He helped her to the limo, gave one last wave to his brother and they were on their way.

Sam dozed off in the limo, she didn't realize they were not going to her apartment; Nick had a surprise for her that she never suspected. The limo came to a stop and Sam sleepily opened her eyes, "Are we home?" he smiled at his sleepy bride, "Yes my love we are." He stepped out of the limo, turned to help her out and waited. Sam stood there staring at the most beautiful house she had ever seen. "Where are we Nick?" He swept her up in his arms, "We are home, baby, we are home." She was speechless, he carried her through the front door, "Well what do you think?" Sam still couldn't speak; she looked around at all the furniture, the fireplace, the window dressings and the spiral staircase in the middle of it all. "When did you have time to do all this?" "I didn't, Jan had a crew of very good people come and do it for me, for us."

They walked around each room slowly, examining every inch. Sam asked if she was dreaming, he just laughed. He took her up the stairs to the master bedroom, he opened the doors to the most romantic suite of rooms Sam had ever seen, she had her own closet and dressing room, there were two bathrooms each with there own shower. Off to the far left of the room was another set of doors, "Do I dare go in there?" He nodded and took her hand leading her to the doors. "Go ahead open them."

When she did it took her breath away, it was a nursery done in teddy bears and balloons. She turned to her amazing husband with tears in her eyes, "You did all this for me and our baby, it is the most exquisite house I have ever seen, thank you, and I love it."

He was aching for her in a way he had never before, "Do you mind spending our wedding night here, Mrs. Naples?" She was so beside herself with happiness she went to him and kissed him, "I was hoping you would say that." They walked over to there bed where he had candles and flowers all around it. Sam was exhausted but she didn't care how tired she was she was going to make this night special for the man who has given her the world. They made love repeatedly that night, every time more exciting than the last. When he finally fell asleep she got out of bed and went exploring their new home.

Down the hall from the bedroom was an office filled with all the necessary things for her to work at home. Next to that was a room filled with fabrics, sketch books and mannequins. He thought of everything for her. At the other end of the hall were two guest rooms, both decorated in soft pastels. She went downstairs to the kitchen; it was bigger than her whole apartment. Cabinets made of cherry wood with ivory colored marble counter tops. Stainless appliances glistened in the morning sun light soaking through the large window above the sink.

She was so elated, she was ready to burst. She ran up the stairs back to the bedroom where she left her love sleeping, climbed back into bed and snuggled up to him. "Thanks Daddy, you were right it is everything you said it would be." she whispered to herself. Sam slept so peacefully in her new world she didn't even hear Nick get out of bed.

When she woke she sat up and called to him, he did not answer, she grabbed her robe, went down the stairs only to find him sitting in the living room. He looked up to see her walking to him, "Morning baby, how did you sleep?" "Like never before and you?" "Me too, are you hungry, I made some breakfast for us." He kissed her and led her to the dining room where he had set up the table full of pastries, fresh fruit, biscuits and hot coffee. Sam was famished; she sat and indulged in everything on the table. He drank his coffee and just enjoyed watching her; she was so luminous he couldn't take his eyes off her. After she had her fill, Sam took her coffee to the sun room; it was a comfortable, cozy room just big enough for them.

The sun was glistening off the small lake behind the house. She was so engrossed in her thoughts she never saw him come in. "Sam, what's on your mind?" "Nothing much, just enjoying the view and wondering how I got so lucky." He kissed her hand, "I think I'm the lucky one Mrs. Naples." They spent most of the day just sitting and talking about the future, the baby and all the things they wanted for him or her. The whole week was spent in their new home, exploring it and each other. When the end of their honeymoon came, they were saddened but ready to take on the world.

The first day back at the design house would be hectic but Sam was looking forward to the challenge of getting her designs done before the fall showing. As they walked out of their home, Nick sighed, "Well here we go Baby, ready or not.

— CHAPTER 13 —

They went to the deli first to see Dom and Margie, hoping that Connie and Grace would be there too. Upon arriving at the deli Sam noticed the sign had been changed, it no longer read "Naples Deli", now it was "Naples Family Restaurant" she was stunned. What was going on, the windows were covered with paper too. Nick all of a sudden jumped out of the car, "He did it, I can't believe it, he really did it" Sam had no idea what he was talking about, but her questions were answered as soon as she walked in the door.

Dom was inside talking to a contractor, the same one Nick hired to do the design house. The whole deli was gone, stripped down to bare walls, no counter, no tables, even the back room was gone. Nick walked over to the two men, shook hands and began talking with them pointing all over the empty shell as Sam watched in amazement. "What do you think, little one, we are finally turning the deli into to a full scale restaurant."

She wasn't sure how she felt about it, it was sad not to have the deli anymore. Connie and Grace came through the door, all smiles, "Well the honeymooners are back, it's wonderful to see you. What do you think about all this?" as she waved her arm around the room. Sam thought about it, "I think it is wonderful for you and Dom. It is something he always wanted to do." She put her arms out to take Grace, Connie handed her to Sam, "Go see your godmother sweetness." She cooed at Sam and held her finger staring at her familiar face.

After Nick was done talking to the contractor he headed for the door, "Be right back" He re-entered the building with blueprints he had in the trunk. The three men went over them, shook hands and Nick took Sam and Grace into what used to be the back room. Dom and Connie were signing something, they handed it to Nick, "What's this" He opened the folded papers with Sam looking on, it was a contract making Nick and Sam partners in the restaurant. Nick wiped his eyes and hugged his brother, "Thank you, this is the best surprise since Sam!"

The two brothers had always planned on opening a business together but until now it just was not possible. Nick turned to Sam, "By the way, I closed down my operation in California and transferred everything here. Staff and all, I never have to go back there again. I sold my house and cut all ties to California, my life is here with you now Sam, and my family." Sam felt so relieved to hear this; she was so worried about him traveling.

As the weeks went on everyone prepared for the opening of the design house, Sam was so busy making sure every line of stitching was right and all the garments were perfect she forgot all about being pregnant. The day of the opening she was sitting in the office finalizing some designs for the holiday line, all of a sudden she felt a twinge, then another, she put down her pad and put her hand on her belly, she was so petite she was already showing. Nick walked in with papers for her to look at, he saw the look on her face, "Sam are you alright?" Sam smiled, "I just felt the baby move, twice." He put his hand on her belly and felt a little kick, his face lit up, "I guess our baby is excited about today too." He bent over to her belly, "Hey little one, hold it down in there so mommy can get her work done." She caressed her belly and the baby calmed down, "Must be the sound of your voice, She has calmed down." "She, you mean he" They both grinned and went back to work.

The day had finally arrived and the first ones to arrive at the opening were Dom and Connie, they brought Margie with them. They gushed over all the beautiful fabrics and designs that Sam had done. All night people were coming in and complimenting them on all the hard work they had put in to the building and wishing them well. Nicholas stood up in front of everyone, "Ladies and Gentlemen our first showing of our designs is about to begin."

Everyone sat down, the first model came out and Sam was pleased with the response she got from their guests. Each model, each design was unique, Sam made sure of that. After it was all said and done and the building was empty Nick brought in a bottle of grape juice for them to celebrate with. "To us, may we be as successful for years to come as we are tonight." They clanged their glasses together and drank to the ending of a perfect day.

The next few months were busy with orders for Sam's designs, coming from all over the country, even some from Europe. The restaurant was almost ready to open, just a few final touches to do. Dom and Connie planned the opening to be before Halloween and it looked like it was going to happen. Nick was so busy with meetings setting up shows for Sam's designs he hardly ever saw his brother. One night around 7 pm Sam and Nick were just finishing up in the office when they heard someone yelling to them from the front door, it was Dom. "Hey up here Dom." He waved at them and walked up to there office.

They were as glad to see him as he was to see them, "Long time no see little brother, just wanted to bring you a copy of the announcement for the opening of the restaurant." Nick was thrilled, "It's a great looking announcement, and we will definitely be there. Sorry I haven't been around much but things have been so busy since we opened I haven't had time for much of anything." Dom understood perfectly, his life had gotten the same way, "I hope you can come to see it before the opening, it is everything we wanted and more." "We will, I promise." With that said they all walked out together and said their goodbyes.

Sam was quiet on the way home, thinking to herself how she missed seeing Dom, Connie, Grace and Margie. "Something on your mind, Sam?" She looked at him with sadness in her eyes; he knew what was bothering her because it was bothering him too. As they pulled in the driveway he promised himself that he was going to take care of it. He understood how close Sam was with his brother and his family; she needed to have them in her life more. She had lost so much in her life before him; he had to make sure she never felt that way again.

He opened the door to their quiet home; Sam immediately went upstairs without saying a word. Nick picked up the phone, called Dom, then called Margie, when he was done with his plan he went to the kitchen and began making dinner. He waited for Sam to come down but she never did, he went upstairs to check on her. He looked in the office, no Sam, he looked in the bedroom, no Sam, he opened the doors to the nursery, and she was sleeping in the rocker he had custom made for her, setting right next to the babies' crib.

She looked so peaceful he hated to wake her, he gently rubbed her arm to wake her, "Baby you need to wake up I have a surprise for you and it will be here soon." She opened her eyes and stretched, "Nick I am so tired can't it wait till the morning?" He was sure she would love it so he was persistent in waking her and getting her ready. She was resistant to his efforts but he did not let that stop him. Finally she gave in and got ready for his 'surprise'. She was getting uncomfortable with the weight of the baby; she never thought it would be so hard to carry a baby. She made her way downstairs to the living room, as she walked in her whole mood changed.

She could not believe she was seeing Dom, Connie, Grace and Margie all in her home. She lit up like a Christmas tree. They all hugged and talked till Nick came in and escorted them all to the dining room. He had made a feast for the family to enjoy, "My love you are so full of surprises and you always know just what I need." Sam smiled at him adoringly. The evening was a complete success; Nick gave everyone the tour of the house, "Little brother you have a gorgeous home for your family to live in and what a family it is." Dom patted him on the back as they went back to the women. Margie was feeling the baby move around when they walked in, she had never felt that before. The three women giggled like school girls, Nick signaled to Dom to come to the kitchen with him, he wanted to give the women time to talk and visit alone.

He grabbed a bottle of wine and two glasses, took his brother out to the deck to talk. He missed spending time with his brother, their lives were so wrapped up in their business' they never had anytime for socializing. The two men talked about their dreams coming true and making sure that their dream of being a close family never gets away from them, they agreed no matter what they would get together once a week just for fun. It was a deal neither one was going to break, it was very important to them both.

Dom heard Connie calling for him, "Well I guess it's time to call it a night." he went into the house followed by Nick, the three women were saying there good byes, the men hugged each other remembering their deal. As the car pulled away Sam turned to Nick, "Do you know how much I love you?" He nodded, "I do believe I do." They went up the stairs hand in hand and climbed into bed.

— CHAPTER 14 —

It was the week of Halloween and the restaurant was ready; Nick and Sam left the office early to go see it. It was the most elegant restaurant they had ever seen. The whole dining area was done in old world Italian décor. The kitchen was huge, big enough for a dozen cooks to work in. They were so impressed they told Dom he was a miracle worker, he took a run down building and turned it into the prettiest restaurant in town. "Well I had a lot of help, but thank you." He was very proud of his accomplishment. He introduced all the employees to Sam and Nick, "These are your other bosses and they just won't be here as much as I will."

They all greeted each other; one of the waitresses' looked at Sam, "Aren't you Samantha Naples?" Sam nodded to her, "I have one of your designs, and it is my favorite dress! My father bought it for me; he said it was made just for me." Sam was so happy to meet someone who owned one of her creations and loved it. "Well thank you, I am so glad you like it, the new holiday line will be out before Thanksgiving, come by and see it." The girl was thankful for the invitation and agreed to bring her father too. Everyone was so excited about the opening; all the employees were preparing their stations for customers. The aromas coming from the kitchen were heavenly; Sam had missed the smell of Dom's cooking. It felt so good to be around it again, Nick noticed how she was enjoying the aromas, went into the kitchen and came out with a plate for her, "Here you go Baby, dig in." Her mouth was watering just looking at it, "It's a little piece of heaven."

They sat together while she ate, Nick discussed what had to be done in the morning for the design house, and she just nodded and kept on eating. He almost laughed at her; she looked like a child with her favorite treat.

The next day was the opening of the dream two brothers had since childhood. Nick went to the restaurant while Sam went to the design house. Sam noticed a stranger in the showroom, she paged Jan to find out who it was, "He is a buyer for a major department store in Europe. He would like to talk to you about your designs." Sam agreed to see him in her office as long as Jan was there too. He walked in the office with Jan right behind him, "Mrs. Naples this is Charles Lawrence from France." Sam shook his hand and asked him to sit down with her. He explained how her designs are all the rage in Europe and his boss wants to sell them exclusively in his stores. Sam was flattered but she explained she could not make that decision with out Nick, her husband and business partner. Jan agreed that was best, Mr. Lawrence said he would be in town for a couple more days and left his card for her, she thanked him and he left.

Jan returned to the office after seeing him out, "I don't think Mr. Naples will agree to this do you?" Sam looked at the card on her desk, "It depends on how many stores he has in Europe." Nick was a very crude businessman; he looked at all sides of a deal before even thinking about it, that is why they have been so successful. Sam went out to the showroom and told Jan she would be at the restaurant if she needed her, she was hungry and she wanted to see how things were going.

When she got to the restaurant she couldn't believe her eyes, it was packed with customers. All the people who came to the deli were there and even some people she never saw before. The people she knew spoke to her and told her how wonderful this place was; even some people she didn't know spoke to her about it. She was listening to a couple from out of town when she felt an arm around her waist. "Well, I see you have met my wife, Sam this is Andrew and Monica from California, we did a lot of business together there. They heard from my attorney about the restaurant and design house and came to check it out; hopefully we will be doing business again."

Sam thanked them for coming; just as she was turning to walk away she got very dizzy. She grabbed Nick's arm and he led her to a seat in the back. "Baby are you ok?" he was scared, he knew she was doing to much and pushing herself to hard but she was a stubborn woman and would not slow down. He called Jan, "Mrs. Naples will not be in for the rest of the day, and would you handle things for her?" "Yes sir, not a problem." Nick went over to Dominic and told him what was going on and that he was taking her home, Dom assured him they would be fine go with Sam, take care of her it was more important. He picked her weak body up and carried her out the back door; he didn't want to make a scene in the dining area. He put her in the car and covered her with a blanket he kept in the back. She was asleep before he got in to drive; he was so concerned about her he drove as fast as he could to get her home.

He pulled up to the house and gently carried her in; he took her straight up to bed. After getting her settled he went downstairs to the kitchen and made himself coffee, when it was done he went into the sunroom, he had to call the doctor for her but he didn't want to wake her, she is so exhausted. He called the doctor anyway and asked him if he could come out to the house to see her, maybe in the morning, the doctor agreed to be there at 8 am before his office opened. Nick felt a little better knowing the doctor was coming, but he was still scared for her and for the baby.

Sam slept the rest of the day and into the night, Nick carefully got into bed next to her. She moved closer to him and went right back to sleep, he lay there wondering if all this work was hurting her and the baby, she is seven months along and till now she had no problems. He dozed off for a while, only to be awakened by the phone. "Mr. Naples, this is the nurse at Doctor Green's office, the doctor wondered if he could come a little earlier to see your wife he has a patient in the hospital getting ready for delivery and he needs to be there with her by 8am." He told her that was fine, thanked her and hung up the phone. Sam woke up and was listening to him, she was glad he called the doctor; she worried so about the baby. "Thank you for calling the doctor for me, I wanted to but I was so tired I just passed out."

He kissed her cheek and went to make her breakfast. He returned with a light meal for her, morning was tough time to get her to eat so he just brought her fruit and biscuits with juice and coffee. She had gotten dressed by the time he came back but he still made her sit in the bed and keep her feet up. He put the tray on her lap and went to get himself some coffee. The door bell rang at exactly 7 am; the doctor came in and went directly up to Sam.

Nick waited downstairs, pacing around nervously, finally the doctor came down. "Well, she is fine and the baby is doing well, but she needs to slow down and rest more. If she doesn't she takes a chance of early delivery and the baby is not big enough to be born yet. She is so petite; I fear the baby will be too." Nick listened closely and agreed to make her slow down; he walked the doctor out and went right up to his wife. "Well, I guess you will be working from home a lot sooner than you planned." Sam started to argue with him and he would not hear a word of it. "I will not let you take a chance of hurting yourself or our baby, and that is final, no more discussion about it. I will bring all your things home for you and Jan will be in constant contact with you. If I have to hire you an assistant here at the house I will, in fact I think that is the best idea. Someone to help you out and make sure you are not over doing it."

He went to her office down the hall and called Jan, he made all the arrangements for Sam to be home. Jan would even take care of hiring an assistant for her. Sam was irritated about this but she knew he was right. She had two more months to go and did not want to take any chances.

The transition went smoother than either of them thought it would, Jan was a god send she was so efficient no one at the design house even questioned what was going on. Nick stayed with Sam for the first couple of days to help her adjust, and then Jan came over with her new assistant, a young girl from the school of design in New York, Angela Frostmen. After all the introductions Nick took the girl downstairs and explained to her what was expected of her. The girl seemed intelligent and very willing to work, he was still concerned, this girl was young and eager but Sam could run right over the top of her, even at seven months pregnant. He needed someone else to be there to and he knew exactly who. He told Jan he would be back in a while, he had to go pick something up.

Jan stayed and oriented Angela to the way Sam liked things done, she explained that if she worked out here she may have a job in the design house when she graduates. Angela listened closely, she did not want to miss a thing, Sam came in and sat in her chair, she listened while Jan took care of everything. Soon Nick was back, "I figured Angela will have her hands full helping you with your work so I brought someone to keep an eye on you and the baby to make sure you are not over doing." He stepped off to the side and Sam was so pleased to see Margie was there.

Who knew Sam better than her and no one was more of a mother to her than Margie. "But what about Dom and the restaurant?" Sam questioned him. "Dom was great about it; Connie's mother is here for at least a year so Connie is taking Margie's place at the restaurant. She was thrilled to do it and they both said you better listen to the doctor, you are in charge of making sure their niece or nephew is born healthy." Sam was so elated with all this help and to have Margie back, that was a bonus.

— CHAPTER 15 —

The holiday line was almost complete; Nick went to the office each day and took care of things there while Sam did her designing at home. He was going through some papers on Sam's desk and found the card left by Mr. Lawrence. He asked Jan what it was; she explained what happened on that day Sam took ill. Jan had called the man and told him that as soon as Mr. Naples had a chance he would call him.

Nick was intrigued, he did some research and found out this man represents the biggest stores in Europe. He called him in France, he apologized for the delay in contacting him, the man was very understanding, he had a wife and kids too. Nick talked to him and invited him back to see the holiday line; he agreed to come back in one week. They hung up and he jumped up and yelled, he was beyond excited, Jan had never seen him like this before. "Jan do you know what this means, Sam will be known world wide." Jan was so surprised by this reaction, "Sir, I am very pleased for you both." Nick went on to explain to her how it feels to do something like this for someone you love so much. She listened to him watching his face light up every time he said her name. Jan was almost jealous of Sam, to have a man love her like that is a dream come true for any woman.

He asked Jan to lock up he was going home to tell Sam about this. He took out of there like he was on fire; Jan smiled to herself about it and got on with business. Nick whistled all the way home, he was so proud of Sam and all she had accomplished and this news would complete her dream. He ran in the house to the office, he startled Sam,

"Nick what is it, are you crazy running up here like that." "Baby, listen to this."

He explained the whole story to her like a kid with a new toy. She got excited listening to him. When he finished he scooped her up and swung her around, "Do you believe it Baby, you will be known world wide." Sam was stunned at the reality of it. Angela was excited for them, "Congratulations, Mrs. Naples. That is terrific news." Margie heard all the ruckus and came running up the stairs, "Miss Sam are you ok?" "Yes Margie I am wonderful." She told her what had happened with the European buyer and how Nick had called him today. She was overjoyed for them, "Miss Sam that is the best news since the baby." She hugged her and helped her back to her chair to rest. "Sam do you think you would feel up to going to the restaurant to celebrate?" She nodded, "Angela and Margie too." They all got into the car and went to celebrate their good fortune.

Connie saw the car pull up and ran out to see what was wrong. "Sam are you ok? What are you doing here?" Sam just smiled; "Nick brought us all here to celebrate" she was confused but helped her into the restaurant. Dom hurried over to them, questioning just like Connie, Nick explained it all to them with the same excitement as before. They were so proud of them they told everyone in the place and gave each customer champagne on the house.

The celebration went on for about an hour when the phone rang; Dom answered it and listened closely. He hung up and called Nick over to him. The two of them spoke for what seemed an eternity, Sam was watching them, something was wrong, why were they looking so serious. Nick came back to the table, "Sam, that was the sheriff on the phone, it seems there was an accident in Montana and a woman was killed." Sam wondered what business this was of theirs, "Apparently, David has been arrested for murder and they want you to make a statement against him for what he tried to do to you. I'm sorry to tell you this tonight." Sam smiled at him "I will, only if it puts him away for good." He was surprised at her, but very proud too. He called the sheriff back and told him to come to the house in the morning, he agreed. The celebration ended soon after, but none of them let the happiness be touched by the news of David.

Sam whispered to Margie, "If nothing else it will end his rein of terror on women and if I can help with that I will." Margie nodded in agreement, "You deserve peace of mind, Miss Sam."

The sheriff showed up at 10 am to talk to Sam, he brought a court stenographer with him. Sam sat in the living room and talked to them for hours telling them everything about David. "With all the evidence and your testimony it should put him away for good, Mrs. Naples; thank you for your help." Nick walked them to the door and they were gone.

Sam felt good about what she did and it showed on her face. She kissed Nick and went up the stairs to work, singing to herself. She knew one day she would be able to pay him back for almost destroying her but she never thought it would feel so good.

— CHAPTER 16 —

The holiday line was finished; Angela and Jan had made sure it was perfect, just like Sam would. It was time to start the spring line ideas, she wanted to get at least part of it done before Christmas. She started sketching, looking out the window at all the snow, it was so sparkly, like little villages twinkling in the in the moon light. She had a lot of work to do before the baby came. It was almost Thanksgiving, her first with Nick, she knew it would be special, everything with him is.

The weeks flew by, Mr. Lawrence bought the whole Holiday line and they had orders coming in by the dozens for the spring line. The design house was closed for Thanksgiving weekend. Nick felt holidays were to be spent with family not working. They had the whole family over for dinner, Dom and Connie, Baby Grace and Connie's mother. Of course Margie and Jan were there too, everyone had a wonderful time.

That weekend they decorated their house for their first Christmas together in their new home. The tree he bought was huge but it fit the house perfectly, "We have to let it stand for a day so all the branches fall in to place, then we can decorate it." Sam was thinking of having Dom and Connie over for a tree trimming party, she told Nick and he thought it was a great idea. They intended on having people over during the holidays, dinner parties and Santa for all the children of the employees. It was to be the best Christmas ever.

The three weeks till Sam's due date were going by so quickly she almost forgot the day was coming with all the Holiday events going on. She was working as often as she could, for as long as she was allowed by Nick. He was getting very watchful of her in the last few weeks. He knew Sam was pushing to get things done but he was afraid she would push herself into an early labor.

He was right, December 9ᵗʰ, 16 days early she started having contractions. She never told Nick till she was finished with the last sketch for the spring line. "Nick, it's time to go, the baby is coming." She stood, bent over at the top of the stairs holding her large belly. He yelled to Margie, "Call the hospital Margie, tell them we are on our way." Margie got so excited she fumbled around the desk looking for the number. "I found it Mr. Nick," she yelled to him as he carried Sam out to the car. He waved to her and they were on their way. Margie paced waiting for Dom to get there for her; she called him right after the doctor. Finally he arrived and she ran to the car, they were not far behind Nick and Sam but it felt like it to Margie. "I hope we make it before the baby is born Mr. Dom." "We will, don't think for a minute I will miss this." He was almost as excited as he was for the birth of Grace.

He had to drive carefully, the snow was building up on the roads, but he was a good driver and Margie trusted him completely. When they got to the hospital he saw Nick's car sitting in front of the door, still running too. Dom laughed out loud, "He must have been really crazed to leave his car here. I will drop you at the door and go park, then I will take care of Nick's car. Go ahead I will be up shortly." Margie got out and hustled in to the hospital, "I am here for Mrs. Naples, and can you tell me if the baby is here yet?" The nurse smiled at the frazzled woman, "Mrs. Naples is in room 315 West and the baby is not here yet, but you can go up to her room." She told her how to get to the west wing and pointed out the elevator to take, just then Dom walked in, "Mr. Naples how nice to see you again, your brother is in room 315 west with his wife go ahead up." He grabbed on to Margie's arm and off they went.

When they got there they heard Sam moaning, they waited to go in till she was quiet. They peaked in the door, Nick and Sam were holding hands, and they both looked so scared. Dom walked in first, "Hey little brother how you holding up?" Nick smiled at him, "Glad you could be here Dom." Dom started to chuckle, "I parked your car for you, I figured you had your hands full and just forgot." They both laughed about it, Sam rolled her eyes at him, "You would think you were the one having this baby." He grinned at her, "I would if I could to spare you the pain you are in my love." Another contraction was starting so Dom left the room with Margie. "We'll be in the waiting room, let us know when it's over." Nick nodded at them and went right back to helping his wife.

Hours went by, Margie was getting concerned, "Don't worry; the first one is always the longest labor. She is doing fine." the friendly nurse from downstairs was standing in front of her; she was brought in to help the doctor. The weather was keeping his regular nurse form getting there. "I will be back to give you news as soon as I know anything, help yourselves to coffee, its right around the corner." They thanked her and went to get coffee, Dom stopped at the nurse's station to use the phone, "I better call my wife she is waiting to here from me and I don't want her to worry."

While he talked to Connie for a few minutes; Margie was pacing in the waiting room, praying for Miss Sam and the baby. Just as Dom came back into the waiting room Nick came out, he took off his mask revealing the biggest smile they ever saw, "It's a girl, we have a daughter!" They all cheered and hugged, "How is Miss Sam, is she alright?" Margie was concerned for Sam, she is so petite and her belly was so big, "Sam is wonderful, exhausted but wonderful." Margie looked up to the ceiling, "Thank you god."

After telling them all the details he could he went back to the delivery room. Dom called Connie with the good news, she was thrilled for them. Margie tugged at his arm when she saw Nick back in the waiting room pacing, Dom turned to see his brother walking back and forth, and he looked worried. He went to him, he put his arm around his shoulders and they spoke for a minute, Dom busted up laughing, patted his brother on the back and fell into a chair looking amazed. Margie was scared to know what was going on, was something wrong? "Mr. Nick is there something wrong?" Nick turned to her with tears in his eyes, "Wrong? No Margie, we have twins, a boy and a girl, Sam never told me. She delivered the boy while I was out here before."

He looked stunned he could not believe he had twins, Margie screeched with joy, "Two babies, twice the blessing." "I better get back in there before I find out we have triplets, I never know what to expect with my wife." They all laughed and he was gone. Dom could not believe it,

Sam never told anyone, she is full of a surprise that's for sure. The sun was coming up, Dom had to go get Connie to come and see the babies. He told Margie he would be back in a few hours she told him not to hurry the weather was bad, she would wait right there. He went out to the elevator and he was gone, Margie got comfortable she knew she would be waiting a while, she dozed off in her chair, and it had been a long night, full of surprises.

The nurse gently tapped her on her shoulder, "The babies are in the nursery if you would like to see them." Margie awoke quickly hearing this news, "Oh my yes" they walked together to the big window in front of the nursery. Right in front, all bundled in their little plastic beds were two of the most beautiful babies she had ever seen. Her eyes filled up with tears of joy, she stood and watched them sleep, and it wasn't long before Nick joined her.

He looked exhausted but he was glowing with pride, "So what do you think of your grandchildren?" Margie looked at him with question in her face. "Yes Margie, you are their grandma and I know they will love you like Sam and I do." Margie was shocked at his words, "I already do love them Mr. Nick, and I would be honored to be their grandma." They stood together for the longest time just watching the twins, pointing at every movement. "Have you named them yet?" Margie asked, "Yes, my wife wanted to name the girl and I named the boy, she is Nicole Marie and he is Dominic Christopher. What do you think?" Margie agreed they were perfect names for them. As they continued to watch these two miracles they were joined by Dom and Connie.

Nick told them the names', Dominic was so proud to have a nephew named after him, he cried at the news. Connie was beside herself with joy she cried and hugged Nick. They all went to see Sam; she was groggy but happy to see them all. Connie whispered to Sam, "You are very sneaky Sam not telling anyone that you were having twins." Sam grinned at accomplishing her surprise. The nurse came in and told them that Sam needed to rest they would have to leave. They all kissed her good bye and she snuggled in her bed and fell asleep.

The next few days were hectic, Nick had to get the nursery ready for an extra baby, Jan helped him get it all set up and ready for their arrival. It was so beautiful he had two of everything; he ordered complete wardrobes for each of them. People were sending gifts to the house; so many he had to turn one of the other bedrooms into a toy room. Sam was coming home in the morning, he had to make sure everything was set, when he finished the last little detail he looked around at all they had done and he was pleased.

— CHAPTER 17 —

Sam walked into the house holding Nicole and Margie was holding Dominic, Nick followed with all her flowers and her bag from the hospital. She went into the living room and sat down, sighing with relief. "I am so happy to be home." She looked down at her daughter and smiled, "You are beautiful, little one and your brother is so handsome you both take my breath away." Nick stood by her busting with pride, "She wants her daddy to hold her." She gently handed her to him; he took over to the Christmas tree, telling her all about how wonderful her life was going to be."

Sam watched him with so much love she felt her heart would burst. Margie gave little Dominic to Sam, went to the kitchen and made Sam some hot cocoa and scones. She brought them into the living room for all to enjoy but made sure Sam got the first one. Sam was elated to see that Margie never forgot about the favorite things from her childhood. She knew the children would have the best times with her just like she did. Both children fell asleep in their parents arms, Nick took Nicole upstairs and Margie took Dominic while Sam rested on the couch. It was going to be the best Christmas ever Sam thought looking at the beautiful tree, Nick came up behind her and kissed her neck, "Tired?" she nodded and he carried her up to bed. After tucking her in he went to the nursery and kissed both the children, "Sleep tight my blessings." He quietly left the room, went down to the kitchen to get a snack.

He took his plate to the living room; Margie was in there just staring at the tree. He sat by the fireplace looking into the fire, they were both so filled with joy they didn't even speak.

In the morning after getting the twins fed and bathed Nick made a few calls to hire a nanny for the babies. Margie over heard him talking and would not hear of it, she would take care of the babies for them. Nick was not sure that it wouldn't be too much for her, "It is so much to ask of you, are you sure?" Margie told him it would be her pleasure to care for the twins just like she did for Miss Sam; in fact she looked forward to it. Nick agreed hesitantly, he told her if it gets to be too much he would hire someone to help. She accepted that much but knew she could and would do it alone.

On Christmas Eve Sam and Nick gave Margie her gift. She opened the box to find papers inside; she took them out to read them and started to cry. They had papers drawn up to make Margie the twins' legal grandmother. She couldn't believe it, Sam and Nick had made her life more than she had ever dreamed it could be and she loved them as if they were her own children. "I don't know what to say, I am so touched that you want me to be a grandmother to your beautiful children." Sam hugged her "Who else would be the best grandma in the world." She smiled at her and wiped the tears from her cheeks.

Christmas was everything and more than Sam ever imagined, Nick spoiled her with jewels and furs, she gave him something he cherished from his childhood and thought it was gone forever, a necklace that his father had worn ever since he could remember, Sam found out from Dom about it and called his whole family trying to track it down, finally his cousin told her it was in a safety deposit box in the bank that Nick always did business with in California. She called his attorney to see if he could get it for her, he was happy to help. Nick and Dom's father had put it in this bank hoping that when he passed Nick would find it; he knew how much Nick admired it and wanted him to have it. Unfortunately, he never had a chance to give Nick the letter explaining where it was. Their cousin she talked to was the one who took their father to the bank, he was sworn to secrecy about it until Nick's father passed away, then forgot all about it till Sam called him. Nick opened the box Sam handed him, he rubbed his eyes in disbelief, he looked at her and stared at the necklace, "How did you know?" Sam smiled at him, "Do you think you are the only one who can do the impossible" He put the necklace on right away , went to his wife, hugged and kissed her repeatedly, "You are some special woman Samantha Naples, I love you so much."

Margie entered the room with both the children, one in each arm, "I think these little ones want to have Christmas too." They each took a baby from her and sat by the tree opening gifts they had for them. It was a perfect day.

— CHAPTER 18 —

The next few years' things got very busy, the restaurant was booming, the design house was busier than ever and the twins were growing fast. It was Sam's dream come true, she didn't think anything could make it more perfect. While sitting in the office, Jan came in with a telegram for Sam, she opened it, and her face went pale, "Oh my, I have been nominated for designer of the year! Do you believe it Jan, me Samantha Naples" Jan was not surprised she knew how hard Sam worked and all her designs were exquisite.

Sam called Nick and told him the news he couldn't believe his ears. He rushed to the office, picked up his wife and danced around the room with her. The awards would be in May, just before the fall line fashion show.

"Samantha, we have to go NOW!" Nick was so nervous about tonight, Sam was so wound up in getting the final touches taken care of for the show she didn't have time to get nervous. She was gorgeous in her Sapphire blue gown, the neckline was off the shoulder, she accented it with a diamond necklace Nick had bought her and it fit her petite body to a tea. He exhaled heavily at the sight of her, took her arm and they went out the door with everyone wishing them luck.

As they sat in the huge auditorium filled with designers from all over the world, Nick could not sit still, Sam was too preoccupied with the upcoming show to notice all her competition around her. The host of the evening was ready to start presenting awards, he read a list of designers that anyone would be proud to be a part of, when he got to

Sam's name everyone applauded. Sam was almost embarrassed about it; she was just doing what she loved to do, design clothes.

Then when he read her name as the winner Nick had to help her up. She was absolutely stunned to hear her name as designer of the year, she went to the stage, accepted the award and spoke of a dream she had always had as a little girl and how Nick made it come true. "I love you Nicholas and thank you" he blew her a kiss from his seat and she walked off stage to flashing cameras and reporters asking questions. He stood back and watched her with admiration, remembering the first time he saw her, the first time he loved her and how it all did work out so wonderful.

He had found the woman he was meant to love; when she was done being interviewed she waved to him to come over to her. "I can't believe this is happening, it's all because of you Nicholas Naples, my only true love. You have filled my life with so much joy, so many surprises, so much love; I can't wait to see what the next 50 years will bring." Nick smiled at her, kissed the lips he knew so well, "Let's go home and see the twins and maybe start that next 50 years with a brother or sister for them." She beamed at him in agreement; they walked out the back door hand in hand, happier than they ever thought they could be. He helped her into the car, kissed her cheek and quickly went to the driver's side.

The anticipation of getting home and seeing the twins, being in her arms and celebrating her success was such of a distraction to him he never saw the truck coming to the left of them.

The phone was ringing, Dom jumped out of bed, looked at the clock, it was 2 am. "Hello, yes this is he" Connie came to him; he was silent as tears ran down his face, "I'll be right there." He looked at the scared face of his beloved wife kissed her, "I have to go to the hospital, there's been an accident and Nick and Sam are hurt badly. He grabbed his clothes and quickly put on his coat, "I'll call when I know anything." And he was gone.

Connie called Margie to let her know what had happened, but hung up after two rings, she decided to go to her and tell her in person. She immediately woke her mother and told her, she kissed Grace in her sleep and was gone.

By the time she got to Margie she had already gotten a call from the hospital, she was sitting in the living room praying for her family. Connie went to her, the two women hugged and cried. After what seemed like forever, Dom finally called "its bad baby, real bad, Nick is unconscious; he's got a lot of internal injuries too. They are trying to stabilize him for surgery." Connie sat listening to him tell her about what happened, "Dom what about Sam? How is Sam Dom?" He was silent for a moment, he began to cry "She didn't make it, she's gone, our little one is gone." Connie screamed and dropped the phone, Margie grabbed it, "Mr. Dom please tell me my Sam is ok" "I can't Margie, I can't." The two women sat and cried for hours, how could this have happened, they were so happy, they had the perfect life.

Margie composed herself, "I have to tend to the children, and I have to fulfill my promise to my Sam." She left the room, went up stairs to the nursery to check on the twins, looked at the two sleeping children she had grown to love so much, "Your mommy will be with you always, you will never be alone." She kissed there heads and went back to Connie downstairs.

They heard a car pull in the driveway, it was Dom, he looked lost, his face was sad. He came in the door, grabbed the two women and cried, "Nick didn't make it, he's gone, their both gone."

— CHAPTER 19 —

It was the hardest funeral anyone in their small community had ever attended. Two caskets side by side, flowers everywhere, Dom and Connie sat next to the caskets with Margie and the twins. Dom was numb; he could only nod to the people who spoke to him. Connie was so distraught she couldn't speak at all. Margie tended to the twins and graciously accepted condolences from all the mourners; she knew she had to be strong for the children. At the cemetery the judge who performed their wedding, performed their funeral service. He was visibly upset, "We have lost two wonderful people, and both were kind, caring, loving individuals. The tragedy that took them from us will never be forgotten and neither will they." He could not say anymore, he walked over to Dom, hugged him and left the cemetery. Everyone there was beyond any consoling.

Nick and Sam had come to be a large part of the community, Margie stood by the caskets, "I loved my Sam, she was the daughter I never had, and Mr. Nick was a great man and father. Their children will never know how wonderful they were, or how much they loved them. I hope you will all be kind to them and help keep their parents memories alive, let the children know what we all knew about them, their strength, courage and the great love they shared.

She turned to the caskets, "Good bye my children, be at peace." She kissed both caskets, went to Dom and Connie, they picked the children up and walked to the car. She turned back one last time to see the caskets being lowered.

"Be at peace, be at peace."